Adieu,
Betty Crocker

Adieu,
Betty Crocker

A Novel

François Gravel

Translated by Sheila Fischman

Cormorant Books

Canada Council   Conseil des Arts
for the Arts   du Canada

ONTARIO ARTS COUNCIL
CONSEIL DES ARTS DE L'ONTARIO

The publisher gratefully acknowledges the support of the Canada Council for the Arts
and the Ontario Arts Council for its publishing program. We acknowledge
the financial support of the Government of Canada through the Book Publishing
Industry Development Program (BPIDP) for our publishing activities.
Additional financial support for this translation is provided by the Canada Council
for the Arts and the Department of Canadian Heritage through the
Book Publishing Industry Development Program.

Printed and bound in Canada

LIBRARY AND ARCHIVES CANADA CATALOGUING IN PUBLICATION

Gravel, François
[Adieu, Betty Crocker. English]
Adieu, Betty Crocker/François Gravel; translated by Sheila Fischman.

Translation of: Adieu, Betty Crocker.
ISBN 1-896951-60-0

I. Fischman, Sheila II. Title. III. Title: Adieu, Betty Crocker. English.

PS8563.R388A7413 2005   C843.54   C2004-906517-3

Cover and text design: Tannice Goddard
Cover image: Tannice Goddard, The Full Cup Café, Bobcaygeon
Author photo: Catherine Gravel
Printing: Friesens

CORMORANT BOOKS INC.
215 SPADINA AVENUE, STUDIO 230, TORONTO, ONTARIO, CANADA M5T 2C7
www.cormorantbooks.com

for Marie-Josée

HAPPY HOUR

The trouble with human contacts is that they tend to drag on. You invite friends over for a simple meal and they think you've offered them a Senate seat. They make themselves at home, they fill your living room with smoke, they slowly empty your one and only bottle of digestif while gravely spilling out the courses they've been teaching for twenty years, or the editorials they read that morning, and they don't seem to hear when you wonder aloud if the battery in your watch is defective or if it *really* is midnight. Why is it that people you think are intelligent want to go on talking for so long? It's beyond understanding.

I love my neighbour, but from a distance. I enjoy the company of my friends, but in small doses. For men like me, who are sparing with their sociability, happy hour is the find of the century: no one feels the need to end conversations that often it would have been better not to start, and the evening is still young when you've finally paid your debt to a social life. If the weather is fine you can take a quiet walk along the city streets, go to a movie with your beloved, or simply go home and settle into a comfy chair with a novel — in short, you're finally free to be quiet. If I had to draw up a list of my favourite social encounters, happy hour would be at the top, followed immediately by visits to the funeral parlour: shaking a cousin's hand, swapping the latest family news, and agreeing to meet at the next funeral. Perfection. Meals with friends come third in line, but only on condition that you meet at noon: you get right to the point, you don't drink alcohol, and in an hour, it's done. Businessmen who want to seem productive often summon their colleagues to breakfast meetings. If I had my way, that would be the norm: you'd see your fellow creatures in the morning, or early afternoon if worst came to worst; the evening, then, you could stay home, open a book, and launch a silent conversation with someone who's taken the time to choose their words and who won't take offence if you fall asleep in the middle of a sentence.

"My dear Benoît, you're an old grouch," says my beloved. "Besides, you don't believe a word you just said. When you get right down to it, what you want is to control everything around you."

Let me introduce Patricia, the beautiful fifty-year-old

with greying hair who shares my life, and who gives me such a glorious smile when she's delivering a home truth that way that I forgive her nasty habit of reading over my shoulder.

"You claim that you like happy hour," she goes on, "but what you really mean is happy *half*-hour — if that! And when you get home, it's not so much to read novels as it is to write articles or books, or to prepare your lectures and speeches. You teach all day and at night you write. That suggests a certain craving to communicate, right? Why shouldn't your friends share that craving? The truth is, you agree to deal with your fellow humans only on condition that you get to choose the where, the when, and the how. In other words, on condition that the speaker is always you."

Bull's-eye. Because why should I be free of the minor flaws most teachers suffer from — I who've been teaching for twenty-five years? Yes, I like to be in control; I don't care for competition, just as it's correct to say that my craving to communicate is inexhaustible. It probably explains why I chose university teaching as a career, even though I've always claimed I'm only interested in research.

A career crowned with success, by the way. Ever since I spent a brief time in one of the tiny left-wing grouplets that proliferated during the seventies, I've been interested in organizations. Organizations of all sorts: armies or unions, multinationals or family businesses, symphony orchestras or jazz quartets ... As soon as humans rub shoulders with other humans, they have to adopt rules, most of them unexpressed.

Ditto for ants and gannets, and even for spruce trees, ferns, and bacteria: every form of life requires an organization, and every organization has its rules, though I'm not about to deliver a lecture — I've already been chastised for behaving like a teacher. So — as I was saying, I took an interest in organizations early on, and it was out of this preoccupation that I turned to administration. I studied for many years, then I got a university teaching job that lets me pursue my research. I have to teach, too, that goes without saying, and while the prospect didn't really thrill me to begin with, I soon realized that I had a certain gift for communicating, and I've devoted more and more of my reflections to it: isn't communication the lubricant for every organization — if not its sole raison d'être? I've published a few articles on the subject over the course of my career, before recently branching off into another kind of writing. I wanted to conjure up the memory of my father, who started a store on Saint-Hubert Street. Perhaps you know *Fillion et frères*, the big furniture store for the French-Canadian family? Because my family was involved in that story, I chose to tell it as a novel, and I must admit that I rather liked the experience, even if most of my distinguished university colleagues looked at me with their eyebrows in italics: A *novel*? You're publishing a *novel*??? The few businessmen with whom I associate, however, greeted its publication with a lot of interest, I'd even say with defer- ence: a number of them considered themselves in fact as artists of management, and as a result they saw me as one of

—
4

them. None went so far as to read the novel though: that would have been tantamount to admitting they sometimes had spare time, which in those circles is unforgivable.

All in all, I preferred Patricia's reaction.

"First you wanted to change society," she told me, "then you branched off into corporate studies, then you end up writing a book about your family. Maybe you'll develop an interest in yourself one of these days ..."

You may be right, Patricia. Maybe I'm already there. And it would be perfectly legitimate on the eve of turning fifty. Or I should say on the *morning after* turning fifty. It was to celebrate that dismal anniversary that my spouse decided to invite some old friends, those old dear friends who must have been zebra mussels in a former life: give them a pipe to cling to and they'll put down roots ... Mind you, I'm only saying that because I like to gripe. I'm surrounded by friends, and not one week goes by that I don't thank my lucky stars.

I'm fifty years old and I have a spouse who is also my beloved and who is aging with grace and wisdom, as the saying goes. Thank you, lucky stars.

I'm fifty years old and I have two grown-up children who are blossoming with grace but with not so much wisdom, which is perfectly all right: wisdom will no doubt come later, there's no rush. Again, thank you, lucky stars.

I'm fifty years old and I have a job I like that provides me with a more than adequate salary on the Canadian scale, one that is indecent on the global scale, and pharaonic on the historical scale. I even have a few investments here and there that would allow me, if I wanted, to stop working right away and live on my private income. We could sell this house which is too big for us now, and Patricia and I could spend the rest of our lives travelling, but that doesn't really appeal to me. Visit museums? No, thanks. I've had my fill of arrow-heads and whether they're pre-Columbian or post-modern, they all look the same. I really can't see myself stagnating beside a pool, reading murder mysteries, and ogling bare-breasted girls. I'm not bedridden, after all: I'm fifty years old, not ninety. And I know myself: two days after checking into a resort hotel, I'd track down the manager and give him my observations on how his business is organized, then I'd head for my laptop to write some articles on the subject, and wonder if, all things considered, I wouldn't be better off back at the university ...

To stop teaching would be totally insane. I'm paid to do research on what interests me and to publish articles that I'd write in any case, and I'm even encouraged to travel to places devoid of interest such as Paris, Barcelona, or San Francisco. Not only would I be depriving myself of a salary, an office, and a secretary, but I'd also have to pay for my trips myself. What's wrong with this picture ...

I don't want to change profession or neighbourhood or take a mistress. My only wish is to keep sailing along: give my lectures, meet with students, publish articles, and a few novels too — why not? — and then go for walks or to the movies, and finally return to the beautiful big house I share with Patricia, a house that's wonderfully well situated on a quiet, shady street, practically next door to the university and close to my beloved Mount Royal, where we like to go walking on Sunday ...

Patricia calls me an old grouch but she's ten times more a stay-at-home than I am, which no doubt explains why she chose to be a translator. Every morning she lays out her books and dictionaries and plunges into the translation of a psychology or philosophy textbook, listening to music known to her alone — slow melodies for cello, with arpeggios that stretch out all morning. Concentrating on her words and lulled by the music, she invents journeys without ever leaving her office. She translates from English to French, but I suspect that now and then she roots around in some old book of spells where she finds recipes for bewitchments or for inventing new dead languages.

"I have to know my way around intrigues," she tells me when I'm the one reading over her shoulder. "Without a tiny drop of witchcraft, any translation would be a betrayal."

I wasn't all that surprised: how else to explain how easily she could read my mind, or the fact that she'd cast such a spell over me? Even if I lived another hundred years, there would still be things about her to discover.

I am financially well off then and my health is good, I'm recognized by my peers, master of my own time, and happy in love. And the height of luxury: as this story begins, I'm beginning a sabbatical and I intend to make the most of it to get some rest and spend time on some research projects that are important to me. You'll agree that there are worse fates than mine on this planet.

And yet, there's something not quite right. A kind of slight uneasiness. Nothing dramatic, mind you, don't go thinking that I'm suffering from depression or anything like that, no; it's just a faint discontent. Let's call it an existential vertigo — if that means what I think it does. When I confide this to Patricia, she brings up the empty-nest syndrome and the changes we have to make in our fifties; she's probably right, but only partially. My energy reserves are diminishing certainly, but I no longer suffer from the performance anxiety that haunted me when I was younger, or from the sense of urgency that gnawed at me when I had a whole lifetime before me.

The vertigo was something I first experienced when two airplanes struck the twin towers of the World Trade Center. I felt the earth shake all the way to Montreal that day, and it seems to me that it still shakes a little every evening, at news time, when I wonder what's going to hit us on the head now.

When George Harrison died a few weeks later, I felt the earth shake again and the sky cloud over. I've always thought of the Beatles as my four big brothers, and George was my favourite. Since he's been gone, I feel like Eric Clapton's guitar solo in "While My Guitar Gently Weeps." I've always loved that, and George's gentle way of talking about his pain

— on tiptoe, in a sense, so he won't disturb anyone. Not everyone is that courteous.

A month later, I found out that my brother was getting a divorce. You can tell me I don't know the first thing about dramatic progression and that divorces are as commonplace nowadays as a head cold, but that doesn't make any difference: Yves and Christine seemed like a cast-iron couple, the kind others envy, the couple you always invoke when you're looking for an example of a marriage that works. Nothing is more like an earthquake than a divorce like that: is there nothing reliable on this planet?

Of all recent events, though, I think it's the death of my aunt Arlette that shook me most, and in a totally unexpected way. At first, it was hard to think of a more inconsequential piece of news. I hadn't really known this aunt, my mother's only sister. I'd seen her now and then when I was a child, but I just had an occasional glimpse of her in my adolescence, and I only ran into her once when I'd become an adult. When my cousin Sylvie called to tell me her mother had died, I was speechless: not only had I not known that Arlette was sick, I hadn't even known she was still alive. Come to think of it, I knew a lot more about George Harrison: the papers were full of details about his lovers and his friends, his cigarette consumption, and the development of his cancer. But the papers had nothing to say about Aunt Arlette, whose only claim to fame was the fact that she was hands down the best maker of Rice Krispies squares in her neighbourhood. So why did the death of an aunt I hadn't seen for nearly a quarter of a century hit me so hard?

"Tears produce more tears," Patricia said cautiously. "Sometimes it takes just one little sorrow to make older, deeper sorrows resurface. It's the principle of the wick ... She was a housewife, you said? A plain, ordinary housewife?"

The quintessential housewife. Arlette was the mother they showed you in the schoolbooks that feminists burned — along with their bras — during the seventies. In fact my brother Marc-André used to call her Betty Crocker, and not just because of her cookies: Arlette had the same dress, the same hairdo, the same attitude of a smiling servant as that archetype of the ideal housewife you saw on bags of flour. You couldn't imagine Arlette any way but in a dress and an apron, holding a feather duster, or leafing through *Good Housekeeping* in search of a new way to fold your table napkins or a new trick for getting wax off a cotton tablecloth. Arlette lived in a perfect house, in a perfect neighbourhood, and she had a perfect family: a good husband, two lovely, good looking children who were always clean and well groomed, for whom she made radish roses and celery stalks stuffed with Cheez Whiz. Arlette was the *Degree Zero* of the organization, she was solitude in its purest state, the modern equivalent of the lighthouse keepers or shepherds who were relegated to the hinterland in the past, and forgotten by all in the end.

My aunt had never been anything but good to me. Whenever I set foot in her kitchen I felt welcome, respected, loved. Even though I'd done all I could to look down on her — and never really succeeded. The same with her children: whenever I saw them I fell under their spell, so much so that I lost all critical sense. Then, as soon as I was home, I tried to convince myself that Daniel and Sylvie were pathetic, superficial, inconsequential ...

"Did you really think you were so superior?"

"I had no choice. It was either that or die of envy."

THE PERFECT HOUSE

The neighbourhood where Arlette lived was called Beaurivage Gardens — I'm not making this up — one of those developments that totally transformed Boucherville in the early sixties. Before that, there were very few single-family houses close to the cities. Builders put up either huge estates for the rich, or mass-produced tiny bungalows without foundations, intended for servicemen back from the war, which were called "army houses." Between the two — nothing. What happened in the sixties was an explosion, a tidal wave, sheer madness. Just like the Chevrolets and Cadillacs that every year gained in length and width and chrome, bungalows kept getting bigger, roomier, and more comfortable. The last word in suburban houses — the Cadillac Eldorado of the single-family dwelling — was the

split-level, especially Aunt Arlette's. Picture it: a split-level
in white brick sitting on a grassy knoll, huge aluminum windows, a wide, nearly flat roof that extended into what even
in French we called a carport ... You always entered that
house through the side door, sheltered by the carport. No
one ever used the front door, which was strictly ornamental.
Nor did anyone ever walk on the sidewalk leading up to it,
not even the mailman, who in fact never left mail in the
mailbox, which was also strictly ornamental. Like everyone
else, he went to the side door and handed the letters directly
to my aunt, who'd be waiting for him at the top of the steps.
When he had nothing to deliver, he would wave to her at
the window from where she kept an eye on her part of the
street. No business was allowed in these suburbs, though
they were presented as emblems of North American capital-
ism, but the streets were always full of life: there were
children all over, and milkmen, bread men, delivery men
who wore their uniforms proudly and whom Arlette waved
at when they went by.

You entered her house through the side door, climbed
up a few steps, and that took you directly into the kitchen,
Arlette's kingdom. The countertops were red arborite, the
table and vinyl chairs were red as well — as red as Jell-O —
and everything else was glossy white — sparkling more
brightly than the incisors in a Colgate ad. In those days, when
the man at the paint store sold you enamel, it was the real
thing.

Now let's take a closer look at the red arborite table, and let's suppose that it's New Year's Day, 1960. I'm nine years old. On the table are mountains of radish roses and Cheez Whiz-stuffed celery, a pyramid of Rice Krispies squares, fudge, cheese straws, and best of all and wonder of wonders — sandwiches with the crusts cut off. While the other guests are swooning over the turkey that has pride of place at the centre of the table, a beautiful turkey so uniformly bronzed it could have stepped out of a tanning salon, what fascinates me are the crustless sandwiches cut into perfect equilateral triangles. If anyone had asked me then to trade my mother for Aunt Arlette, I would have said yes without a hint of remorse: the sandwiches at our house always had a double crust and that crust was usually stale.

"You would have traded your mother for Aunt Arlette?"

"We're talking about a nine-year-old child in 1960, don't forget. And if the Montreal Canadiens could trade Jacques Plante and Doug Harvey to the New York Rangers, nothing was sacred. I would have traded my mother for Aunt Arlette any time, yes, without even trying to negotiate 'future considerations,' as they say in the wonderful world of sports. Arlette was a fantastic cook. My mother wasn't. Does that answer your question?"

"Perfectly. You may continue."

When we went to Aunt Arlette's, we felt as if we were living in an American TV series or, even better, in an ad for one. It had nothing to do with wealth or modernity, not even with interior decoration. It had to do with Arlette herself, who played the role of housewife so well that you couldn't imagine her anywhere but in her kitchen, where she always greeted us with a disarmingly candid smile, a smile she would never think of not wearing. It was a matter not of politeness but of personality: displaying a bad mood in public pre-supposes a certain wish to assert oneself, and she probably hadn't enough backbone to want to stand out that much.

The living room was an outright masterpiece. A picture window facing due south, sheer curtains, furniture uphol-stered in red velvet — which came of course from *Fillion et Frères*, the big furniture store for the French-Canadian family — and most important of all, the white broadloom …White broadloom. Can you imagine the upkeep? Needless to say no one ever went into that room. The only thing miss-ing was one of those ropes they have in museums to keep us out. My aunt was the only one allowed there, once a week, to vacuum. Then she would walk out — backwards, so there were never any footprints and the pile of the rug was always straight and even. I never saw the mark of a foot on it, or the print of a bum on the sofa. Anyway, why would we go there? There was no TV or stereo in that living room: they were in the basement, along with everything else of any interest. The only function of that immense living room, then, was to be cleaned by Aunt Arlette.

Outside the living room was a small vestibule that opened onto the front door, and three steps leading up to the other level, where the bedrooms were. I really liked those three steps you had to climb to get to the bedrooms. Especially because one of them was Sylvie's …

"Wait, let me guess. Sylvie's your cousin, the two of you are the same age, she's kind of pretty …"

"She's pretty, she smells good, and she has breasts. For now though, let me remind you that I'm all of nine years old. The crustless sandwiches are a lot more appealing than my cousin's breasts, which are nothing more than vague promises, and I'm a lot more interested in visiting the basement than in looking at the living-room carpet …"

"I've been waiting for that one too. It's often like that in your stories: a secret room, usually in the basement …"

"It's not my fault that rec rooms were always in the basement. If people put their electric trains, ping-pong tables, TV sets, and cousins in attics, I'd have told you attic stories … So, as I was saying, I'm nine years old and I race downstairs where I find Daniel and Sylvie, who are, needless to say, perfect children. How could it be otherwise? Can you even imagine that a family moving into a new house in a new neighbourhood in a prosperous America would be anything but perfect? The height of perfection was the number: *two* children … Both had their very own bedroom, their very own parent, their very own Oedipus. It was quite simply indecent, that's the only word."

Let me make the introductions. Daniel is the man with the eternal smile, if you know what I mean: whatever the era and whoever the photographer, he always displays the same broad, straightforward, open smile, the same bright eyes, the same pleasant appearance. As a child I played hundreds of ping-pong games against him or, rather, *with* him. At first he beat me systematically — he was two years older — but he sent the ball back patiently, gave me chances, encouraged me, taught me his best tricks — always with his signature smile, which made him tremendously likeable. A few years later, when I finally managed to win my share of victories, he was always in a good mood and congratulated me on my good moves, even when they had let me score the winning point. Daniel knew how to lose as gracefully as he won, and there was never the slightest sign of affectation in his attitude. If it's true that games are excellent signs of a person's genuine nature, then Daniel had the healthiest personality I've ever known — or else he was a fabulous actor.

It was Daniel who introduced me to the Beatles. He tried his hand at an electric guitar, without much success, but he had a genuine talent for electronics. He'd assembled some amazing stereo equipment in their basement — by the standards of the time, at any rate. It wasn't a simple turntable, it was a hi-fi system as he said with pride. And on that hi-fi, I heard "Help!" for the first time. Until then I'd only heard the Beatles on transistor radios that sounded like cracked rattles. It's an understatement to say that I wasn't impressed by "She Loves You" … But hearing John sing "Help!" and "You've Got to Hide Your Love Away," and that hoarse voice of his on the very first bar of "You're Going to Lose that Girl" ... It still gives me shivers.

Daniel liked John's voice but he preferred the songs of Paul, with whom he had a lot in common, as it happened: the baby face, the dandy style, the unbearable candour of a person for whom life seemed too easy ... And Daniel's life really was too easy, at least as compared with the Fillion family. Take this example: for a teen in those years to love the Beatles — perfectly normal. For the mother of that teen to like the Beatles too — that certainly was less common, though it did happen: the Beatles were such nice boys, we heard that often enough. But for that mother to sit at her sewing machine to make clothes absolutely identical to what the Beatles wore — now that was exceptional, right? The Cardin collars from the early years, the military jackets from Shea Stadium, even the brass band outfits from the Sgt. Pepper period — Daniel was able to wear all the Beatles outfits at the same time as the Beatles: he was a Beatle in real time, as we say nowadays. So Daniel had a devoted mother who made him all the Rice Krispies squares he could eat, and who also made him clothes that helped him multiply his female conquests ... Admit it, that was a little frustrating.

Daniel lived in paradise and he knew it, which may explain why he never left: when he graduated as an accountant, he set up his office in his mother's basement and never moved. Which is also why he was there when Arlette died. From what Sylvie told me, Arlette simply fell onto the kitchen floor, like a dead leaf falling from a tree. Daniel was in the basement when it happened. He raced up the stairs four at a time, he called an ambulance, but it was already too late. A gentle death, with no suffering. Her heart stops beating and that's that. A discreet death, in the image of my aunt. A dead leaf falls from a tree and right away it's covered in snow.

One day my sister Jocelyne compared moods with the waterline of a ship and I think she was right. Some spend their lives hauling anvils, others have a cargo of ping-pong balls. As for Daniel, he always seemed to have a hold full of helium balloons. A bachelor and happy to be one, a sports car he changed every year and sometimes drove to visit clients … A happy man.

"A happy man who still lives with his mother? That's not exactly my idea of a healthy personality …"

"Listen, I said he'd set up his office in Arlette's basement. I never said that he *lived* there."

"Okay. Let's say he still lives with his mother, but part-time. In other words he's cut *half* of his umbilical cord. A tricky operation."

"Granted. Daniel lives with his mother part-time. Every morning he goes down to his office to work and comes upstairs for his coffee break. Arlette serves him coffee along with a few cookies or a homemade date square fresh from the oven … Daniel chats with his mother for a while, he goes back downstairs to work, then comes back up for lunch. Arlette *prepares* his lunch, she *sets* the table, she *clears* the table, she *washes* the dishes ... What's the grammatical term for a present tense that expresses not only an action taking place while one speaks but also designates a habitual action? That present tense, whatever its name, is perfect for describing household tasks: it's a present tense that never ends. Arlette *cleans* the countertop, Arlette *rinses* her table linen ... Now Daniel will have to learn how to conjugate those verbs in the imperfect, and I've got a hunch it won't be easy."

"What about evenings? What happens when that poor little boy who's fifty-odd years old leaves the house in Beaurivage Gardens and goes home?"

"No idea. I don't even know his address. I've always assumed that he lived in some bachelor pad at the top of some tower, with a view of the St. Lawrence, and that he spent his weekends driving around in his convertible cruising gorgeous girls ..."

"And you say that he's likeable?"

"Yes, I said he was likeable, and I still maintain it: that's an objective quality, one that stems from who he *is*, that has nothing to do with what he *does*. Daniel is handsome, cheerful, and likeable, that's the way it is, we can't do anything about it. Sure, you can sneer at him for the same reasons, but if you want to do that, you should wait till he leaves. That's just plain decency."

Sylvie didn't inherit that natural good humour. She's neither tormented nor easily depressed, let's get that straight, but she's always been more nervous than her brother, less cheerful too. I don't know what she's hauling in the hold of her ship, but her waterline seems to me to be at a normal height. She's always been tall and thin so every dress suits her, and every hairdo, and every necklace — in a word, the whole style invented by homosexuals who can tolerate only women with the bodies of teenage boys. When she was ten she already spent hours looking at fashion magazines and painting her nails. We're the same age, but I preferred the company of her brother; I could play ping-pong with him. Needless to say, I changed my opinion a few years later, when hormones began to complicate my life and I thought I could take advantage of our family ties to engage in certain experiments with her under the carport — wasn't that why God invented girl-cousins and carports? I'll say it right up front: my enterprise was not successful.

For a long time Sylvie worked as a hairdresser, then she changed and became a beautician — electrolysis, facials, treatments of various kinds — you probably know more about those things than I do ... Her business is doing fairly well, as far as I know: Sylvie must have three or four employees, even more, maybe, and that probably explains why she always seems preoccupied. You have no idea how much energy it takes to run a small business like that. Beyond a certain threshold, companies run themselves, so to speak. Tasks well-defined, responsibilities limited. But for a very small business, it's a whirlwind of decisions, many of them crucial: an employee is sick and there goes half your turnover … So Sylvie's not a Rockefeller or a Bombardier or even a Lise Watier, but she's still a businesswoman. She's lived with Jean-Claude for ages, he's a nice guy who works for a courier service …"

"What about the father? Sylvie and Daniel must have a father, don't they?"

"It's true, people tend to forget poor Marcel. Marcel was to that family what Stuart Sutcliffe was to the Beatles …"

"Give me a hint who that was, would you? Do you mean the drummer who was replaced by Ringo?"

"That was Pete Best. Stuart Sutcliffe was the friend of John's, the one who died too soon. A good guy, Marcel … Now shall we devote a little chapter to him?"

THE VOYAGEUR

If I always talk about Aunt Arlette's house, Aunt Arlette's kitchen, Aunt Arlette's living room, it's because Uncle Marcel's life seemed to be lived outside. He cut the grass and pruned the cedars, he washed his car and watered the driveway until it gleamed, and he was probably very glad that men's and women's roles were so well defined that they seemed to have been codified by an unusually finicky union: everything inside concerns the wife, everything outside is the responsibility of the husband, and that's that. Criticize that division of labour all you want, it's hard to imagine any rules that are much clearer. These must have prevented countless conflicts.

Marcel, then, lived outside his house, like any normal man, and more than the average even, because he was a bus driver with Provincial Transport, which was later renamed Voyageur. And voyage he did, Uncle Marcel: Chicoutimi, Gaspé, Toronto, New York, Miami — always on the road, working every weekend and many nights as well. Like my father and so many other men back then, he seemed to be genetically programmed to work and be silent. His worker's skills didn't stop him from being a good father, though, who never came back from his travels without bringing something for his family. Often it was just some trinkets bought at the New York terminus — Bazooka gum, Superman comics — but also more carefully chosen presents: a Beatles record not yet available in Canada, exotic chocolates, cashew nuts ...

Marcel lavished attention on his Arlette, telling her all about his travels and always trying to make her laugh. I remember coming up from the basement once, where I'd probably been playing ping-pong with Daniel, and catching them deep in conversation. They were sitting at the kitchen table, talking about this and that and a thousand other mundane matters, the way friends do. Marcel was animated, Arlette all smiles, and they obviously enjoyed each other's company. The sight of them made a strange, unreal impression on me that verged on indecency.

I also remember seeing them contravene one of the most restrictive clauses in the collective agreement that governed couples at the time: Marcel accompanied his wife to the supermarket, something no real man would ever do — unless he was retired and dying of boredom.

That *voyageur* must have clocked millions of kilometres on North American roads, in snow and rain, but he never had the most minor accident, no fender-bender, nothing. And he died stepping out of his bus. He'd just let off the passengers and was slowly heading for the parking lot where he'd left his car when a delivery truck appeared out of nowhere and hit him. The brakes had failed on the Berri Street hill.

This happened in the early seventies. I'd just turned twenty.

I went to the funeral parlour of course and I remember being surprised at not seeing Arlette.

"She tried, but she couldn't leave the house," said my mother, who'd gone to stay with her sister for a few days to help her during this difficult time. My mother had mentioned a *nervous shock*, saying the words sotto voce as if it were something shameful.

So it was my mother who received condolences on Arlette's behalf, and she also helped her sister send out thank-you cards.

Arlette was always allergic to funerals: when my father died she took the trouble of calling me and all my brothers and sisters to offer her condolences, but she didn't come to the funeral parlour or the funeral. Nor did we see her when my mother died last year. My cousin Sylvie had referred to a malaise — which was perfectly plausible as far as that goes: Arlette was eighty and nearly blind ... Still, it was strange, wasn't it? Cécile was her sister, her only sister, they'd always been like two fingers of one hand ... a hand with only two fingers ...

"Arlette must have had an aversion to funeral parlours," says Patricia. "It's a phobia I share ... What kind of funeral will she have, by the way?"

"There'll be a prayer service next Saturday. No funeral parlour, no viewing of the body. Those were her wishes ... But to get back to Marcel. It's a stupid thing to say, but I've always been convinced that his early death was a good deal for Arlette — as long as you take the word *deal* in the strictly financial sense. The mortgage on the house in Boucherville, which was covered by insurance, was paid off in one go. Marcel had life insurance too and since he died young, and in an accident, Arlette inherited a substantial amount, which in Daniel's hands yielded a profit. Add to that another significant sum — obtained thanks to Provincial Transport, who'd lent the family a lawyer to help them prosecute the delivery company — and overnight Arlette found herself not worth a fortune, I don't want to exaggerate, but with a comfortable cushion that guaranteed her a perfectly decent income. So we have a twentieth-century woman of reasonable intelligence who enjoyed excellent physical and mental health, a woman who was far from being an aristocrat but had nonetheless never worked in her life, never drawn a salary, never had a boss.

"Except for her husband and her son ..."

"If you want. Pretty easygoing bosses though, in my opinion. But then again, no, I don't accept that label: Marcel wasn't Arlette's *boss*."

"True, it's a word that's not used much nowadays. I'd forgotten that we don't have bosses or employees now — we have *partners* or *associates*, who sing a hymn in praise of their company every morning … So was Arlette Marcel's *associate?*"

"Arlette was a wife and mother, that's all. Why split hairs? Wife, mother, and housekeeper. And definitely very good at *management*, as the snobs say in France … By the way, do you remember a book entitled *Madame et le management?*"

"No, not at all. It sounds ridiculous though."

"It's a bad title, granted, but the book does say some interesting things. The author, who was a woman, started with the principle that, like it or not, household tasks have to be done. And since that's so, she explained, let's be efficient and apply sound modern management principles to those activities: output, productivity, efficiency — that sort of thing. Taylorism applied to ironing, if you want. This lets the modern housewife gain some valuable time which she can use for more creative tasks: helping the children with homework, for instance, or making a pretty dried-flower arrangement in a vase so that her husband will be in a good mood when he comes home from work to a house that's sparkling and clean … I'm hardly exaggerating. Still, the original idea was good: as long as one agrees that housework has to be done …"

" … and has to be done by the wife …"

"That was the weak point in the structure. The book was very successful in France and Belgium, but you can imagine the welcome it got here! This was during the seventies, if I remember correctly, and the author came to town here during her promotion tour. First of all, her publicist hadn't come up with anything better than to deliver her into the claws of the most aggressively feminist radio host, who of course made mincemeat of her. If memory serves, the poor author left hastily, after taking refuge in her embassy ... But still, if she'd titled her book *Housework and Management* or pointed out that it was intended for *the househusband and/or housewife*, the way we do now ... But I don't think there's anything shameful about wanting a clean kitchen and knowing the secrets of storing woollen clothes ... Why shouldn't that be a goal as noble as making a fortune or winning the Stanley Cup? Some people dream of hitting the lottery jackpot or finding the philosopher's stone, others want to find the Golden Fleece or their G spot, still others dream of learning how to calculate the squaring of the circle or recomposing Beethoven's *Ninth*, or exploring space or destroying Carthage, or going west, young man ...While Arlette wanted her kitchen countertops to be clean. And why not? Why shouldn't happiness, which we look for everywhere but at home, be found in a split-level in Beaurivage Gardens?"

"You left some out," Patricia replies. "Several, actually."

"What?"

"You can also want to reach the inaccessible star that's invisible to the eyes, to find both your healthy weight and your inner child, to take the road less travelled while trying not to drown in a bowl of chicken soup for the soul ..."

I love the way Patricia sometimes lets me talk nonsense and I love it even more when she joins in. And that was how, by enumerating the great quests of humanity, I got a terrible hunch: Arlette's kitchen had been a labyrinth from which she'd never found the exit. And I walked into it too. I even got lost there, I think.

FROM THE OTHER END
OF THE LINE

When Sylvie called to tell me her mother had died, she asked me to pass on the news to all my brothers and sisters. I pick up the phone around ten o'clock Sunday morning to fulfill my task. At noon I'm still at it.

I start with Marc-André. In situations like this, he's the first one I call. Marc-André has always been resolutely family. For a long time his children were the centre of his life and he played the father role to perfection: a nice house in Longueuil close to the nature park, two magnificent children whom he ferried to the pool or the rink, an equally magnificent wife, a blond dog that ran across the grass — the works. Marc-André has made a success of his family and he's proud of it. And so he should be. So he was a happy king in his suburban palace, at least until his children grew up and started university. Because having four cars was out of the question, Marc-André traded his lawn for a condo in the Plateau, but I suspect he still longs for the time when he carted the kids to the pool and the rink. In the Fillion family there's an aggressive determination to make a success of their families and proclaim it to the world at large.

So I phone Marc-André to give him the sad news: Betty Crocker is dead.

I give him time to swallow the news, then we spend a few minutes reminiscing about things that come back to us in a jumble: the electric train, the ping-pong table, the Jell-O red kitchen, the living room broadloom, the New Year's Day dinners, the death of Uncle Marcel ... I soon realize that Arlette's family wasn't as important to Marc-André as it was to me. My brother never played ping-pong with Daniel, never fantasized about Sylvie's breasts — and our Sunday afternoon visits to Aunt Arlette bored him to tears. We may be brothers but we don't have the same reliquaries. We go on reminiscing, but without too much conviction, then we agree to go to the funeral together.

Next I call Christiane.

"Arlette? ... It may sound stupid but I thought she'd been dead for a long time ... Give me the address of the funeral parlour, I may drop in if I can find the time."

From the tone of her tone of voice you know that she won't.

Yves isn't home so I leave him a message. It's unlikely that he'll be shattered by the news of Aunt Arlette's death, not

Yves: he's in mid-divorce, which gives him plenty to worry about. (Don't let lawyers get involved, Yves. Do whatever you want — as long as you don't call a lawyer!)

I leave a message for Louise as well, and I'm delighted that she isn't home. I've always preferred talking to her by voice mail.

Jocelyne I keep for last. First, because she's a psychologist and always has something interesting to say when you get her going on the family, and then quite simply because she's my favourite sister. By keeping her for dessert, I can take my time.

In a perfect world, everyone would have access to a Jocelyne. My big sister listens the way girls listen when they have that talent, and she knows me as well as if she'd created me herself. Still, I haven't been able to take advantage of her as much as I would have liked. She followed her first husband to Toronto and stayed on there once she got unmarried. It would have been hard for her to abandon her clientele and start again from scratch, especially since she'd been plying her trade in English for more than ten years. As we both had careers to build, marriages to make successes of, and children to raise, we lost sight of each other for years. My Toronto sister had become almost a stranger.

All that changed when my mother died. We'd had to talk on the phone often to deal with matters related to the estate, and of course we used those talks to try to harmonize our respective memories; finally we got in the habit of calling one another just to talk, so that today I'd have trouble saying whether Jocelyne is first of all my sister or my friend. In any case, I have no desire to ask the question: she's there and nothing else matters.

Jocelyne has often told me that working in English gave her an advantage: linguistic and cultural differences let her see things in a different light, gave her a critical distance, a new way of seeing problems. I think I understand what she means: for me, talking on the phone has always been equivalent to using a foreign language. With her at the other end, I catch myself talking in another way, tackling problems from another angle.

"I've got bad news, Jocelyne. Arlette is dead."

Jocelyne registers the shock, then she carries on with some memories, pretty much the same ones that figure in my own and Marc-André's anthology: the New Year's dinners, the perfect roast turkey, the white broadloom in the living room ... Then I mention the crustless sandwiches and the Beatles records, but she quickly leaves that topic and moves on to our mother's strange relationship with her sister.

"Arlette was the ear at the other end of Mama's voice."

Arlette's phone calls ... Torrents of memories come tumbling down.

In my childhood home in Saint-Lambert, there was just one telephone for the whole house — a black dial model fastened to the kitchen wall. To me as a child the phone was for a long time an exclusively female device, like the sewing machine or the curling iron; so it was normal for it to be in the kitchen. Never did I see my brothers use it, my father even less.

My mother called Arlette every day, sometimes more than once. Any excuse was good. Besides being an ear, as Jocelyne said, Arlette seems to have been a domestic encyclopedia, the Yellow Pages, and a world atlas all in one. Did Cécile need to know how to remove tea stains from her china cups? She'd call her sister: Arlette knew those kinds of things. How to get rid of midges in the rhododendrons, what to do with leftover ham, how to make a buttonhole in synthetic leather? Arlette knew everything, absolutely everything. Ever the informed consumer, she knew the best places to find fresh coriander or dried mushrooms, and she could tell you that laundry soap was cheaper at Steinberg's than at Dominion that week, but that blade roasts ...

If one of us wanted to know the best route to take to Sainte-Agathe or Sherbrooke, my mother would call Arlette, and our aunt would open one of her road maps that let her follow every moment of her husband's journeys, covering in inches what he did in miles. You could always count on her to know how to get from Montreal to New York or Philadelphia, or from Boucherville to Pointe Saint-Charles by car, or from La Prairie to Joliette by public transportation. As a child, I imagined that Arlette's kitchen must look like an airport control tower, with all kinds of radar and warning lights and monitors, and that her kitchen table was always strewn with maps and bus schedules, pencils and compasses. I was always surprised when I went there to see that her kitchen table was bare, her countertops spotless, with no sign of a gigantic filing cabinet hidden in a corner that was filled with every piece of information imaginable about anything that might be useful to someone, some day. There was nothing like that in Arlette's kitchen, yet Arlette knew all the answers, like some autistic people who can tell you instantly that in the year three thousand and fourteen, November 12 will fall on Wednesday (and don't forget your winter tires, Arlette would have added, at that time of year the roads in the Parc des Laurentides are liable to be icy).

Arlette always knew everything, then, and Cécile phoned her every day, so that my brother Marc-André once suggested, as a gag, that they replace the telephone with two tin cans joined by a wire: since you only use the phone for talking to Arlette, you'd save money ...

That was the day when Marc-André learned that there are subjects you should never joke about, and one of them was Arlette.

Arlette wasn't just an expert on itineraries and stain-removal. Above all, she was a confidant — an ear, as Jocelyne puts it — and no doubt the only ear that was always available to my mother.

If my mother suddenly stopped talking when I went into the kitchen, I knew she was on the phone with Arlette (who else?) — and that she was sharing *confidences* with her, a word that has always rhymed with *silence*. She'd change the subject then — and not very subtly — while I was opening the fridge to pour myself a glass of milk, then she'd start talking again in an undertone, sometimes even cupping the phone with her hand so her remarks would land in Arlette's ear and nowhere else.

When the silences were weighty and my mother's voice more solemn, I knew she was talking about my father.

But other times I'd hear her talk about her children, and then her voice was happy and spontaneous, as if the words were being carried by birds: she would say with pride that Marc-André had got a hundred in geography, that Yves had won his First Class badge in Boy Scouts, that Christiane's piano teacher had said she had perfect pitch, and so forth. These remarks were all the more surprising because she would never have spoken them to her offspring: like most pre-Dr. Spock parents, she thought that compliments would spoil children as surely as candy would spoil their teeth. From that point of view, her educational mission was a total success: I'm here to tell you that no one got spoiled. For some obscure reason though, she seemed to forget that principle when she was talking to her sister. If we wanted to hear ourselves being praised, or even just talked about, we had to creep into the kitchen when our mother was speaking to Arlette — in other words nearly any time. When I heard her say that I'd got ninety in math or that I'd come home from school with a bruise or a splinter, I felt as if I was the main topic, that I was a star. Of course it didn't last: as soon as she realized I was there, my mother would change the subject. Which probably explains why I came down with a few cavities all the same, by accident.

There was another more roundabout way to find out that our mother really had said something good about us to someone. If we went to visit Arlette in the following days or even in the following months, our aunt always had a kind word for us.

"I hear that you got ninety in math. Congratulations! Too bad about your French exam though …"

I would look at her, stunned: I'd forgotten about the French exam — since the day after, in fact. Not only did Aunt Arlette remember, she didn't forget what mark I'd got and the teacher's comments … How could she keep it all in her mind? And why was *she* the one who congratulated me or sympathized with me? It was enough to make your head spin. Flustered, I would race downstairs where Daniel was waiting for me to play ping-pong.

THE FINAL CONFLICT

I was twenty-five when I saw Arlette for the last time. That was a quarter-century ago, but it seems to me that it goes back much further. It was at the height of my leftist period, when I spent most of my time demonstrating, handing out newspapers at factory doors, and going to endless meetings. That period left me with a deep loathing of meetings, which in turn allowed me to publish some articles that brought me a certain renown during my early years of teaching. In them, I showed that only rarely do meetings bring solutions, but that they actually encourage conflicts: if we have to get together it's because there are problems and if there aren't, we'll invent some. The multiplication of meetings and committees is a sure sign that an organization is in decline. The efficient business should therefore reduce them to the minimum.

From that time I also recall a method of investigation based on the use of linguistics to determine the various hierarchies in companies, a method I still recommend to my students: first, ask to meet with the big boss of some organization or other, and note his or her favourite expressions, tics, obsessions. After that, you just have to stroll around a variety of the company's departments and you'll quickly spot the parrots who pass on those key words to the lower levels. You can launch one of those expressions yourself, along the lines of *decision-making parameters* or *operational synergy*, for instance — it doesn't matter if it means anything or not — then follow the progress of that expression day by day, thereby bringing to the fore the company's communications networks. Plumbers do the same thing when they inject smoke into your pipes to spot leaks.

I got a book out of that, entitled *Periwigs and Parrots*, which is still cited twenty years after publication. I like to think that its success was due not only to the title, which I was quite proud of. "Periwigs" was a reference to the court of Louis XIV, an excellent model of decadent organization precisely because of the prominent place given to the parrots. My hunch was this: any business with more than fifty percent parrots on its staff is in danger of ossification. But if it has less than twenty percent, watch out: the business lacks cohesiveness. I applied the model to the study of five large

Canadian banks, with convincing results.

I'm getting off topic, I know, but apparently I still have to convince myself that my activist years weren't a total waste of time.

As I was saying, then, I was twenty-five when I saw Arlette for the last time. I was a convinced revolutionary so I had absolutely no reason to have anything to do with this aunt who would be parked forever in the suburbs of History. It was as a favour to my mother that I went to her house.

"Would you drop in at Arlette's on your way?" she had asked me. "I've bought her this part for her sewing machine, it won't be too big a detour..."

I had no good reason to refuse, so I went.

So here I am, behind the wheel of my yellow Datsun, driving along boulevard Marie-Victorin towards Boucherville. My car is full of smoke and suppressed anger (I smoked like a chimney back then), and my briefcase contains — along with the part for the sewing machine — some books by Lenin and some Marxist newspapers. And I ask myself: Should I take advantage of this visit to my aunt for a little propaganda?

A brief moment's reflection and I decide not to try convincing Daniel of anything whatsoever. How could he — a superficial, insignificant little accountant who drives around in a convertible and is still waited on by his mother — be sensitive to the revolutionary cause? It would be pointless to waste my breath on him, for sure. But Arlette? She obviously can't be numbered among the advanced elements of the working class, but she is a woman and a housewife and there-fore a twofold victim: surely there must be a touch of anger I could stir up. Maybe she could get involved with a group demanding free and accessible abortion, or daycare centres for the people, or a food bank?

The closer I get to Beaurivage Gardens, the more I feel at once ridiculous for thinking I could make Arlette into a revolutionary and guilty at giving up before I've ever started. Something's wrong.

I just have to see the house, the immutable white split-level, and to spot Arlette's silhouette at her kitchen window, where she's been watching for me, and my last resolutions drop — if I still had any. I'm not twenty-five years old now, I'm ten, and I'm coming to visit Aunt Arlette, who's so nice and who makes such yummy Rice Krispies squares.

Here I am under the carport, and now I'm fourteen: it's here, right here, that I came within an inch of kissing my cousin not so long ago.

I open the door, I climb up the four steps to the kitchen, and now I have no age. Time has stopped, as it always does the minute you set foot inside that kitchen. Arlette is ageless too, she always looks like those illustrations of the perfect housewife in our schoolbooks, always in the same dress and the same apron, which go so well with the red-and-white kitchen. I wonder why science fiction writers rack their brains in search of scientific justifications for the crack in the space-time continuum when we experience such phenomena every day: in Arlette's kitchen, nothing ever changes, neither the Jell-O red countertops nor the sparkling walls nor the vinyl chairs that go *psshhh* when you sit on one.

Arlette offers me coffee and a slice of pie, then she bombards me with questions about my brothers and sisters.

"Has Jocelyne finished her university courses? Your sister is such a good listener, I'm not surprised that she's going into psychology, though she could have done whatever she wanted, definitely, a talented girl like her ... And your sister Louise: she won all the spelling bees, her dictations were perfect, so it's no surprise that she's a proofreader, you're so lucky to have all those talents ..."

I said that Arlette bombarded me with questions, but that's not quite the right word. Rather, I have the impression that she's reciting a lesson, that she's taking an exam.

"Marc-André is married, his wife's name is Marie-France, she's in insurance, like her father ..."

The only thing I can say is, *yes, right, ten out of ten, perfect*, or just nod, and each confirmation seems to fill her with joy — or at least reassures her. Encouraged, she goes on telling me about my brothers and sisters, even giving me details that I didn't know.

"I hope your brother solved his trouble with the water seepage in his basement. I talked to Daniel about it and he thinks it's not a problem with the foundation, but the ground level, sometimes the earth has a tendency to subside ..."

Arlette is speaking but it's my mother's voice that I hear.

I always used to think that what was said into a telephone wasn't really intended to be heard, especially not that much. How is it that my aunt has remembered everything, why does she stockpile such useless information, and why does it matter so much to her that I confirm it?

I talked about it with Sylvie a few days after the funeral.

"Your impression was right," she told me. "Without knowing it, you were giving her an examination. She had an unhealthy concern for details, and it would have broken her heart if you'd caught her out on even one. You can't imagine the things she knew: if you'd asked her, she could have rhymed off the birthdates of your brothers and sisters, the schools they attended, the names of their teachers, the number of days they missed when they had mumps, the name of the dentist who extracted your wisdom teeth ... She never forgot a thing: a week before she died, she could have told you what you had for dinner on Christmas Eve in 1966 ..."

"How did she do it? Did she take notes? Keep a diary?"

"Not even. She was just very focused, that's all. Those things were extremely important to her. They were her whole life. Ten years after the event, she could have told you what colour tie you wore at your first communion ..."

"Why hold onto all those details?"

"I don't know," Sylvie answered, shrugging. "I imagine it was part of her illness ..."

Now hang on. I'll talk about what Sylvie calls Arlette's illness in the next chapter. Just now, I'm still twenty-five and

I'm polishing off my apple pie while I listen to Aunt Arlette tell me about my brother's problems with water seepage in his basement, said brother having never bothered to inform me about it.

Soon Daniel comes up and joins us.

"Excuse me," he says, "I was on the phone with clients ..."

Arlette pours him a coffee without his asking. It's coffee time, I imagine, and the servant knows his habits ... The accountant is served like a pasha, he is the very essence of male chauvinism, but even so I can't hate him. Arlette seems to be happy to serve her son, and Daniel's smile is a universal solvent that melts away all ideologies. I gab with him for a while, I take a second piece of pie, then I give the sewing machine part to Arlette, who thanks me again and again, as if that part could save her life.

It's nothing, Arlette, really, it's nothing ...

I make my way to my yellow Datsun, my head full of questions: why do I feel obliged to hate Daniel but can't? A socialist society would need accountants, right? Maybe even insurance underwriters, when I think of it, though that merits more reflection. And because there'll always be a need to bake apple pie (at least I hope so) and to brew coffee, why is it so hard to imagine a library in which Mao's philosophical essays would be shelved next to *Good Housekeeping*?

Yes, I did ask myself questions like that. The more I think back, the happier I am to have a good memory. It lets me be glad I'm getting older.

I asked myself questions like that, and I missed out on everything else: Arlette was interested in us, Arlette knew everything about us, but we never asked her for anything. Arlette had at her disposal thousands of pieces of information about my family, yet she never passed judgement ... As a rule I was insensitive to others, I freely admit that, but how can I explain that I never asked Arlette any questions, not even out of simple courtesy? How can I explain that the thought of asking her opinion about this or that or even just asking how she was never crossed our minds?

"She'd certainly have been surprised," Sylvie told me when I asked her. "She would have been genuinely surprised and she'd have quickly changed the subject. She didn't think that she herself was interesting."

She is still standing at the window, waving to me as I get in my car ... I wave back: Adieu, Arlette. Adieu, Betty Crocker. Adieu, silent image.

Don't notice me, said the image, above all don't notice me, please, act as if I don't exist.

ARLETTE'S ILLNESS

Marc-André and I are the chargés d'affaires in the Fillion family. Wills, funeral arrangements, property management, tax returns — we handle all the thankless tasks with responsibility and detachment, as devoted sons and efficient administrators. We're amply rewarded — as much by our good conscience as by our inalienable right to represent our family at the social events that involve it. In other words, we get stuck with the funerals. For us, it's not a burden; on the contrary.

So there we are, my brother and I, in an enormous, brand-new funeral complex, and we're thrilled that the multinational that absorbed the old Quebec family-owned funeral business at least preserved the French name of the venerable institution. It was of course an excellent business decision: who would entrust the remains of a loved one to a branch of Colonel Sanders?

But never mind their nationality and their motivations, I have to say that the owners did a good job: the funeral complex is a vast concrete building — apparently you can't build with anything else nowadays — but the carpets are clean, the woodwork sober, the rooms big and bright, the staff discreet. And you can look as much as you like, there's not a hint of a religious symbol anywhere. When the priest comes to give his sermon in a while, he'll seem like an intruder. Times have changed.

Daniel and Sylvie greet the visitors, who include some of their clients and friends, two or three old ladies I don't know who I assume are neighbours, some brothers and sisters-in-law of Arlette's who've come all the way from New Brunswick. It's obviously nothing like the funeral of Victor Hugo, but there are still a fair number of hands to shake and condolences to exchange, so we can't chat as long as we'd have liked with Sylvie, who was telling us about Arlette's illness.

I have just said that we're always surprised at the number of people who show up at funeral parlours, when Sylvie makes this seemingly trite remark.

"It's especially surprising because Arlette never went out."

"You mean she went out *rarely*," says Marc-André, quick as a flash — and I'd like to elbow him in the ribs to let him know that this is not the time to correct what seems to me to be a minor exaggeration.

"It's not a manner of speaking, though," my cousin replies. "Arlette *never* went out."

"Come on, Sylvie: you mean she never, ever went out?"

I must look as if I'm what my father used to call hard of understanding, but the information can't work its way into my mind — into Marc-André's either, for that matter, judging by the questions we ask in turn: She never went out to get her hair done? To see the doctor? Go to the bank? Do her grocery shopping? Get some fresh air?

"I know it seems weird to you, but to us it was perfectly ordinary. I cut her hair, Daniel looked after her finances. As for grocery shopping, she phoned in her orders or asked Daniel to go. She ordered her clothes from Sears or made them herself. When she had no other choice, she'd ask Cécile … Cécile never talked about it?"

I look at Marc-André and I'm sure we're thinking the same thing: Sylvie's exaggerating, she's pulling our legs.

"She must've gone outside to hang out her laundry, didn't she?"

"She didn't cross the street, she didn't set foot on the sidewalk in front of the house, she didn't step under the carport, she never opened the door, not even to pick up circulars stuffed behind the aluminium decorations: Daniel did that. She *did not go out*, period. Since my father died, she didn't set foot outside, or even her little finger."

"She never got treatment for that?"

"We'd have had to persuade her to leave the house. In the

old days Papa could, but it was always very hard. He took her to see a psychologist two or three times, but she hated it ..."

"So she did go out ..."

"When Marcel was alive, she did agree to go out now and then, but it was an adventure every time. He had to be with her all the time and he couldn't let her out of his sight. They'd do the shopping together, always in the same place, they parked the car in the same lot, and then they went up and down the aisles in the same order, never retracing their steps. When Papa died, Daniel offered to take her to the supermarket but she refused. She preferred to phone in her orders or she'd ask us to go ..."

"So ever since your father died ..."

"Papa died in 1970. I don't have to remind you of the circumstances. Or remind you that it wasn't something that would encourage Arlette to go out."

"So she didn't leave the house for more than thirty years ... Thirty years!"

"Yes, thirty years. It may sound totally crazy to you but I think Arlette was actually healthier than most of the people I know."

A priest appeared and interrupted us, asking us to go to the chapel, where he dished out his propaganda.

"We were all scattered," he reads with difficulty from the sheet of paper he holds in a trembling hand, "and now the death of ... (he straightens his glasses) of ... Arlette ... (he tries to straighten them again but his left hand trembles even

more than the one that holds the paper, which doesn't help)
and now the death of Odette Desmarais ..."

The Catholic church is experiencing serious recruitment
problems, but that's no reason not to listen to its official
representatives: an organization that has perpetuated itself
for two thousand years deserves our respect, and it's in that
spirit that I try to pay attention to what he says, but I can't.
While he tries to persuade us that Paulette is not really dead,
in spite of appearances — so are we to conclude that we are?
— my mind is combing the countryside — or maybe I should
say the kitchen, the kitchen where Arlette shut herself away
for thirty years ... Thirty years of cleaning the countertops
and scouring the oven, thirty years of making coffee for Daniel,
thirty years of being posted at the window, watching life
go by ... During those thirty years, I lectured in the four
corners of the world, I went diving in the Caribbean and
hiking in the Grand Canyon, I swam in the cool water of
Laurentian lakes and I skied in the Rockies, I went out to
movies and restaurants, I visited family and friends, I went
out to buy bread at the corner or even for no reason at all,
simply to get some fresh air, I walked on countless sidewalks
and paths, on grass and snow, sand and pebbles, I wore all
kinds of shoes, boots, and sandals. And all that time, Arlette
was content to pace the linoleum in her kitchen and vacuum
the white broadloom in the living room ... Why, Arlette?
Even cloistered nuns must take the air sometimes. Even the
worst criminals aren't locked up for that long, they're

allowed to walk in the prison yard and they're out on bail before the end of their sentence. No one stays shut up inside for thirty years, it's inhuman. What crime did you commit, Arlette, to warrant such a punishment?

"Now let us pray for the rest of the soul of Claudette," says the priest, his voice quavering more and more, "of Pierrette who will always live on in our hearts."

Odette, Claudette, Pierrette, why not Bobinette the marionette while he's at it? Her name is ARLETTE, I want to shout at him, her name is Arlette and it's not all that complicated, *Monsieur le curé*, you could at least take the trouble to learn her name before she disappears completely. Her name is Arlette, that discreet woman who is now nothing but a heap of ashes placed in a wooden urn that looks like a miniature coffin. Her name is Arlette, that woman who never had a job, never belonged to a club, an organization, a group, that woman who spent her life shut away in a suburban kitchen and is resting now in a little box that's even smaller than her kitchen ...

Maybe the old curé knew what he was doing, I thought on my way home. Odette, Paulette, Claudette, Pierrette: maybe his prayer was meant for all those housewives shut away in the kitchens of their suburban houses, all those forgotten women outside of time. But the name of this particular woman is Arlette, and I don't want her confused with another.

FREE CONSULTATION

$\mathcal{A}$s soon as I'm home from the funeral, I call Jocelyne to tell her about Arlette's illness, about her supermarket expeditions with Marcel, about the window she hardly dared to touch, the circulars that Daniel had to take away, and the more I tell, the harder it is to believe myself. Something about it is beyond my understanding, something I can't assimilate, something that words, even repeated, can't resolve. Try to imagine it, Jocelyne: Monday the same as Tuesday, Tuesday the same as Friday, and so on for thirty years. Thirty years of never seeing the trees that have grown on the north side of her house, for the good and simple reason that none of the windows gives onto that side. Picture Arlette's seclusion, her capital boredom, imagine her fear, imagine her loneliness.

"Housebound wife," says Jocelyne as if she were thinking

out loud. "I don't know how to translate that into French: *l'épouse en garde à vue, la ménagère prisonnière* ... No, *prisoner* seems too strong, unless you make it clear that she was her own jailer and that she was the one who'd installed the bars."

"*Housebound wife*, you said? Is that the clinical term?"

"It's a classic variant of agoraphobia. If you only knew how many clients who ..."

"Wait a minute: isn't agoraphobia fear of crowds?"

"Not really. It's more like a fear of being afraid. A kind of permanent anxiety, a prison you lock yourself into. It's a disease that feeds on itself, like paranoia: the more you shut yourself away, the more afraid you are of going out, and the more afraid you are, the more you shut yourself away ... Because it was normal — at one time, anyway — for women to be confined to their kitchens, others didn't notice if they never went outside. Which is where the expression *housebound wife* comes from ..."

"Sylvie is convinced that in spite of everything, her mother was stable ... Do you think that's right?"

Jocelyne's answer is a long silence. I don't hear a thing, not even her breathing, yet I can sense her thinking at the other end.

"If happiness were calculated in kilometres," she says at last, "airline pilots would be a thousand times happier than air traffic controllers. You can find your stability anywhere — including within your neurosis ... 'All human misery

comes from this: man's being unable to sit still in a room.'
Who said that?"

"No idea."

"I don't know either. Maybe Arlette was able to sit still in
a room — in her kitchen, actually — and she found a certain
stability there ..."

"If it were me I think I'd be bored to death."

"Do you think she'd have been less bored if she'd spent her
days in an office and her evenings at the mall? Do you think
the people who hang out in smoky bars are less unhappy?
There's no denying, hers was a serious case, but some phobic
people can be relatively happy in other respects; it's not as
surprising as you seem to think. What intrigues me most
about this story is what went on around her. No matter how
resourceful Arlette was, she still needed allies and it's often
the allies who sustain collateral damage. Dependency is a
game that takes two — or more — to play ... What must it
be like to have a mother like Arlette, who's afraid of everything? Among mammals, it's the mother who transmits the
feeling of fear to her young ..."

"Daniel and Sylvie seem quite sane, as far as I can tell ..."

"Can I call you back in two minutes? There's something I
want to check ..."

When Jocelyne says "two minutes" it really is two minutes.
I barely have time to get up and drink a glass of water when
the phone rings.

"I found the source of that quotation," she tells me. "It's Pascal. Blaise Pascal. And I found a definition of envy: *a feeling of discontent and ill will because of another's advantages.*"

"To whom do we owe that quotation?"

"To a man called Webster. With some minor changes of my own."

"And what made you think it was something I should know?"

"I thought about the little fellow you described to me the other day, looking greedily at some crustless sandwiches, a little fellow who thought that Arlette was a perfect mother, who discovers today that she spent her life shut up in a kitchen … There's a good reason why you're so interested in Aunt Arlette."

BEAURIVAGE GARDENS

Sunday morning, very early. First I make my way to Saint-Lambert, where I spent my childhood, then I retrace the route we'd sometimes follow on Sundays, when the whole family went to visit Arlette. Boulevard Marie-Victorin, which follows the St. Lawrence, the old stone houses of Boucherville ... When I was young, horses would sometimes block our way. Every spring, a Boucherville farmer would load them onto a barge that took them across the river to Île Charron, where they spent the summer in total freedom. When he brought them back in the fall, they'd become wild again.

There are no more horses running wild on Île Charron, but I've heard that there's a population of deer. Aside from that, nothing seems to have changed in the old part of

Boucherville. There are the same stone houses, the same willow trees, the same church, which is very old too … It's a peaceful place that makes you want to slow down. You'd like to go sit on a park bench across from the church, watch the river flow, let a family of ducks that's swimming close to shore come closer … I think about Arlette, who never came here and sat on this bench, never walked along the river that runs so near to her house, never looked at this view that affects me like Proust's *madeleine*. What were you so afraid of, Arlette? How could such a bucolic landscape make you so anxious?

A few more streets and we're in Beaurivage Gardens. During the sixties it was a neighbourhood seething with excitement. Every week there were new streets lined with new split-levels, but none was more beautiful than Arlette's, with its façade of white bricks. I drive slowly past the house without stopping and continue aimlessly through the now stabilized neighbourhood: there's no more new construction, the trees have grown, the streets are deserted. What has become of the children? The street used to be full of them, playing hockey or hopscotch or skipping rope … Gone, those children. Or maybe they're hidden away in their basements, plugged into their Nintendos.

I leave my car near a park and walk. It's a beautiful day, and the neighbourhood is pleasant — as long as you don't have an aversion to the suburbs. Contempt for bungalows and lawnmowers is a very common attitude among some of my university colleagues. I've always thought that a single-family house in the midst of some greenery was a perfectly legitimate and absolutely democratic dream. But if there are no more children and if you can't even take advantage of the trees, what are the suburbs good for? Look at this park, Arlette, it's a simple little park like the one across from your house, but you've never gone outside that house, never touched some bark to see how rough it was, never studied it up close to watch ants climbing; you lived surrounded by trees but to see them up close you'd have had to watch a TV documentary. There were no monsters outside your house, Arlette, just trees, houses, and quiet people who had no ambition but to enjoy the peace and quiet of this suburb. So what were you afraid of, Arlette?

A few more steps and you could have walked under the willows along the Pine River. Not the St. Lawrence, Arlette, a tiny little river visited by ducks and swallows, a river that runs right near your house and that you never saw. You preferred to stay in your kitchen. Where you stayed for thirty years ...

I walk some more along the streets of Beaurivage Gardens, I look at the landscaping, and now and then I even venture a glance at the kitchen windows, in case I might see the furtive silhouette of another Arlette. Soon I can picture an army of Betty Crockers, an army of the shadows, who scrub, sew, clean, scour, sweep, launder, iron, polish, mend, baste, sear, braise, sift, knead — a silent army with no formal organization, but terrifically effective ...

I come back to Arlette's house, that white house I only ever looked at with envy, and I feel feverish as I always do when I'm accumulating information for an article or a book. Feverish and uneasy, not quite sure where I'm going but confident that I'll find something eventually if I let myself drift along with the current, and knowing in advance that I won't be alone at the rendezvous. I need you, Arlette. Need you to read over my shoulder. Need to talk to you, to go back in time till I meet up with that little fellow looking greedily at some crustless sandwiches, that little fellow with sadness settling inside him ... Will you let me go on with my investigation, Arlette? I'll disguise myself as a researcher and I'll be discreet, I promise.

BLIND SPOTS

Sylvie welcomes me to her beauty spa an hour before it opens, two days after her mother's funeral.

"You'll be able to get an idea of what it's like. Monday mornings are always quiet. And this early, we'll be able to talk in peace."

On the stroke of nine o'clock I'm seated in the waiting room while Sylvie makes coffee. She was supposed to show me around, but half an hour after my arrival we haven't left the waiting room. She feels like talking and so do I. The remarks follow one another in a way that defies logic — but who is logical when he's calling up family memories? — and always in a tone that's very calm, detached almost, as if it were following the rhythm of the new age music that seems to have started up automatically when Sylvie opened the door. She answers the phone, jots notes, files papers, but she always lands on her feet and picks up the conversation where she left it, in the same soothing tone. I don't have my sister Jocelyne's talent for listening, but I've questioned enough businessmen and businesswomen in the course of my career that I know how to ask the right questions. And so I adopt the mirror tactic, as interviewers say, and I let my cousin tell me her story, interrupting as little as possible.

თ

You don't become a beautician from love of blackheads, Sylvie tells me right off. Or because you want to rid humanity of unsightly hair. You become a beautician because you need a way to earn your living, because you enjoy the work, but mainly because you like people. My clients are journalists, housewives, teachers, lawyers, I've even got a cabinet minister! It's always interesting to get people to talk about their work: I feel as if I'm taking courses, but a little bit at a time. Sometimes they talk about important matters, sometimes just details, but it's always enriching. It's as if I were taking courses on every subject at the same time, without having to take an exam. It suits me perfectly. I've always loved listening to people, but I've never had a very good memory. Jean-Claude, my husband, has often told me I'd have made a good psychologist: apparently there are people who pay a lot so that other people forget what they've been told. But school and me, well ... Still, I know I'm something of a psychologist in my own way. I apply masks to my clients, I give massages, which relaxes them so that often they confide in me, sometimes they even break down and cry … Have you ever had a mask? You should. It regenerates the tissues, it relaxes you in-depth, really, you should try it. That would be fun, wouldn't it? Why so suspicious? You ought to let your-self go for once …

Hair is important. It's the first thing we see about a person, even if we don't pay attention to it, and like it or not, it has a lot to do with our first impression. I was a hairdresser for ten years, and it was something I liked. When I walked down the street and saw heads that I'd worked on, I felt proud. I wished I could sign them, the way an artist signs a painting. I'd have put my signature on the back of the neck. Just a tiny little *Sylvie* you could hardly see, a tattoo as fine as a hair, people wouldn't have seen or felt anything …

When I was little and played with dolls, I never wanted to punish them or console them, look after them or rock them to sleep. I wanted to dress them but, even more, I wanted to do their hair. I'd curl it, then I'd straighten it, I even figured out how to tint it. You should try tinting nylon, just to see …

I was fourteen when I really started doing hair. Arlette had found a hairdresser who came to the house in the evening, after work. I watched her and asked her questions. She was good at cutting but pretty bad at colouring. Mind you, the products that were available back then were too strong and it was hard to know how much to use … So because Arlette's hairdresser wasn't very good at colouring, she asked me to do it instead. Her hair was fine and porous so it was hard to do, but I loved it. After that, I tried my hand at cutting and I was pretty good, so I became my mother's hairdresser, and believe me, Arlette wouldn't have been satisfied with just anybody. She may not have gone out, but that didn't stop her from wanting to look her best.

Arlette? She was the perfect client: patient, calm, didn't complain, and she always had something interesting to talk about, even though she never went out. She could talk about the private lives of movie stars, the drought in Ethiopia, the US elections ... For her, no subject was unimportant. She listened to the radio all day long, so she knew everything. It's different today, but back then there was more news on the radio, there were interviews, serials ... Today, it's always the same songs. I can't take them. I had tapes of gentle music made, for relaxation, but I don't even hear them anymore. Same thing at home — I don't listen to anything ...

You may find it hard to believe but I don't think Arlette was ever bored. As I said, she loved listening to the radio, but she never just sat there doing nothing. She always found something to keep her hands busy. There were meals to fix, housework, sewing ... Remember the Beatles outfits she made for Daniel? What you may not know is eventually all Daniel's friends wanted them and she made costumes for them too. Everybody started his own musical group back then, it was so funny ... The parents supplied the cloth, Arlette did the sewing. She liked to keep up with the trends so she'd watch *Jeunesse d'aujourd'hui* with us, send me out to buy teen magazines ... My friends were all jealous: they had to buy magazines out of their allowances, but my mother bought them for me! She needed them for her work ... We'd look through them together, we'd talk about cuts and colours, and I adored it. She did too, I think: she made stage costumes for Les Têtes Mauves or The Black Stones, but at the same time she could listen to a radio program about literature or the life of Schubert, or who knows what ... With Arlette, you were never bored.

Just one example: as you know, Arlette studied at the Institut familial, a school that trained girls to be doctors' wives. The nuns were very good at French, apparently, and they were fabulous at recipes for pie crust, but for English, I can tell you they were hopeless — the ones who taught Arlette at any rate ... Mama knew how to say *yes* and *no*, and even that ... Then came along Beatlemania, as we said back then — and you know how much we loved the Beatles in our house — so Arlette had Daniel buy her an English-French dictionary and she translated all their songs, word for word. I'll let you guess what the results were like: *huit jours une semaine, je t'aime* ... That's just to show you how open-minded she was, and she could always come up with things to do. She had her crosswords, her dictionaries, her birds ...

No budgies though. Too dirty. Wild birds, that she'd attract to the windowsill with seed. Your mother would buy it at a store in Montreal, it came in twenty-kilo bags, enough to plant all the fields in a third-world country. There was millet, thistle — everything you need to attract cardinals, goldfinches, all kinds ... She had her regulars, her barflies, as she called them. She wasn't satisfied with calling them by their family names, which she found in her Peterson guide: she gave each bird its own name, and she'd wait for them, year after year ... For Christmas one year we gave her binoculars and I never saw Arlette so happy.

Yes, we always called her Arlette. So did Daniel's friends and mine, no one would have called her anything else. We're going to take some cloth to Arlette, we're going to pick up our costumes from Arlette ... Even better: if you can imagine, our friends sometimes came to the house even if we weren't there. They came to see Arlette. She'd give them cookies and milk, they'd talk, she'd listen. Amazing, isn't it?

All that to tell you that Arlette may have been sick, but she wasn't crazy. I don't know what you hope to find out with all your questions, Benoît, but if you're expecting a portrait of an unhappy woman, well, you've come to the wrong place. As long as she was in her house, Arlette was perfectly normal; I'd even say she was better balanced than most of my clients. She knew more about the world outside than plenty of people who do leave their houses. More than me anyway! When I try to watch the news on TV at night, the first thing I know, I'm fast asleep on the living-room sofa. Jean-Claude has to wake me up so I can go to bed.

You too? That's reassuring. Arlette remembered everything she heard on the radio or TV, everything Marcel told her, everything your mother said — everything. And nothing made her happier than when she was doing something for someone: Papa had been dead for a long time and there were still uncles who'd call her to ask the best way to get to Philadelphia. I don't know what we're going to do with all her roadmaps, in fact, oh God ... It's ridiculous, isn't it? You bury your mother without shedding a tear, then you think about some roadmaps in a kitchen drawer and the floodgates open. I'm sorry, Benoît, I don't know what ...

Sure it's an illness, sure some people are cured, every shrink I've spoken to said the same thing: the person just has to be slowly deprogrammed. So on the first day, she'd put one foot outside, the next day she would sit in a chair under the carport, a week later she'd have walked to the sidewalk ... But you can't cure a person who doesn't want to be cured. And before we'd got to that point, we'd have had to bring up the subject first ...

We'd really have to call her bluff to get her to talk about it. And even then she'd manage to wriggle out of it ... She said it was her allergy: *some people are allergic to cats, others are allergic to peanuts, I'm allergic to outside, now let's talk about something else.* Talking about it made her unhappy, and no one wanted to make her unhappy ...

As for Arlette's illness, in the end everyone forgot about it. She was our mother, and mothers are always normal, right? She didn't drink, she didn't beat us, she was always there, she was even funny, she had a vivid imagination, she was loving … The only drawback was that she asked us to do some errands, but even that was rare. One can always arrange to have something delivered, you know. Arlette was resourceful. And there were Marcel and Cécile, she had a whole network of suppliers, each one did his share …

Sure it's an illness, I'm not trying to convince you otherwise, but she didn't seem unhappy, no more than you or me, no more than lots of other people, and certainly not nearly as much as the celebrities who've got everything their hearts desire and still end up killing themselves. She was the best mother in the neighbourhood, everyone envied us, including you — and don't try to tell me otherwise. For Daniel and me she was normal, she was Arlette, that's the way she was, and so it goes, everyone has their fears, their quirks. Arlette suffered from an anxiety that was out of the ordinary, it's true, but for the rest she was an ideal mother.

When I was a child, even when I was in my teens, I never knew that my mother was *different* as they say nowadays. I didn't even have a teenage crisis, to tell you the truth. Neither did Daniel, for that matter. We knew such things existed of course, we were aware of them, we saw them in movies or on TV, our friends talked about them at school, our teachers of religion practically encouraged us to have one so we'd be normal teens, and Arlette often talked about what went on in your family — just between us, your mother had a rough time, didn't she? Jocelyne, Christiane, Louise — it happened to all of you, in fact I gather some of you aren't over it yet ... What was your problem with Cécile anyway? We didn't understand.

If there's one thing you inherited from your mother, Benoît, it's your talent for changing the subject ...

Arlette could have been bored to death when we were adults, of course, but Daniel kept his office in the basement, so it wasn't all that bad. And she had her birds, her crosswords, her radio programs ... She always found ways to keep busy so she kept coasting along. At one time she took on sewing jobs, rather she subcontracted subcontracts, you know how it works in those circles ... There were mountains of Wonderbra cups and straps in her kitchen and she'd spend her day assembling them. She did that for several years, then she dropped it. She still sewed, but on a volunteer basis. She sewed sequins onto majorette uniforms or figure-skaters' costumes, but often she'd be lambasted by parents who thought their daughters' costumes weren't as stunning as someone else's ... She stopped because of these intrigues, but also because of her eyes, of course. In the end she couldn't really see. She had cataracts and could have had an operation but ...

When she died, she hadn't done any sewing for a long time. She kept busy listening to the radio and playing solitaire, like everybody else. And every morning at ten o'clock, your mother phoned. It was very hard on her when Cécile died ...

How about another coffee, cousin? I've got a couple of calls to make, you can wander for a while, I know you like nosing around. Take advantage of it while the place is empty ...

༄

Sylvie is right, I do like nosing around. It's the first virtue of a researcher and one that I always try to stimulate in my M.A. students. You're fascinated by power and you want to know what the real decision-makers think? Perfect. First of all, throw out their autobiographies: they're nothing but lies and platitudes from the pens of ghostwriters with no imagination. Instead, get a job as a caddy or a cleaning lady, look at their hands and fingernails, the crease in their pants, the height of their heels, find out what model of car they drive: everything has something to tell you, even the way they decorate their offices — an anonymous place if ever there was one. Note how thick the carpet is, the direction the windows face, the signature on the painting on their wall, examine their gold pens and wonder if they've ever used them, look at the photos of their wives and children, and you may discover that appearances can be deceiving and that the attributes of power resemble the tattoos on our young delinquents: the more scared they are, the thicker they lay it on.

I look at the receptionist's desk while Sylvie listens to her phone messages. Steel-grey countertops, halogen lighting, a bright red vase, dried flowers ... The combination of techno-chic and psycho-pastel works: it suggests a medical clinic as much as a psychologist's office, you feel that you're in good hands and so you can let yourself go.

On the glass shelves set into the wall, a collection of moisturizers, exfoliating creams, and regenerating lotions … Apparently steel grey is all the rage, as is the Greek alphabet. Particles, molecules, energy: they play the scientific card, even though there's something religious about the environment. New age music has replaced the organ, chemical perfumes have supplanted incense, you leaf through women's magazines instead of missals … In Sylvie's clinic, the magazines are recent, a detail that's not insignificant: who would entrust her face to a beautician who's one season behind on trends? I check out a few magazines: sex and shampoo, sex and curls, sex and perfume, sex and bathroom decoration — a dozen infallible ways to drive him wild in bed, six new gadgets for masturbating at work … Why should men feel guilty about looking at *Playboy*?

Sylvie calls a client.

"Tomorrow at eleven," she says in a professional voice. "Yes, Madame Turcotte, that's perfect."

She hangs up and automatically resumes her cousin-voice.

"It's not for love of blackheads that you become a beautician, no … When I was fifteen I already knew how to do streaks, permanents, everything. I was an excellent hairdresser — I could have shown my teachers a thing or two. I was a hairdresser for ten years and I could have kept at it longer if I'd wanted. Madame Patenaude, who owned the salon where

I was working, was going to open another one in Longueuil, and I could have been the manager ... I toyed with the idea for a while, so much that I ended up changing professions: I didn't want to just work with hair till the end of my life. It's too hard on the back; I kept getting tendonitis and, well, Longueuil isn't the end of the world, but since Jean-Claude is always on the road we'd have had to buy a second car, while here I was close to home, close to Mama too ...

"It was important for me to live close to Arlette, yes, but why should that be a problem? True, I had to go there to cut her hair, but it wasn't an obligation, lots of hairdressers go to their clients' houses you know, and living in Boucherville or Longueuil — what difference does it make?

"I was part of Arlette's network of suppliers, that's right. Each of us had our specialty: Daniel's was the grocery shopping and the dry cleaner, and he looked after the house; I took care of her supply of ... of feminine products, shall we say; if a sewing-machine part broke, Arlette would slip into the conversation that she needed something, and Cécile would go shopping for it. She put herself out a lot, you know ...

"No, it wasn't really an obligation. I never felt as if I were paying a debt. It was just normal, that's all. I helped Arlette, but she also helped me. It was an exchange. Besides, she was my mother after all ...

"In Boucherville, new developments were going up every day, I was sure I'd always have a clientele if I opened a spa. I talked it over with Jean-Claude and he agreed to invest in my business. We scraped some money together, Arlette helped out, Daniel too. It was tough in the beginning, but now I'm doing well, as you can see. And it's all mine. I own the building, I have six employees — that's the hardest part, I can tell you. There's a big turnover so I spend a lot of time training new girls. It's hard, but I enjoy it, I like people ... Can I ask you a question, cousin?"

"Of course, cousin."

"Why does it seem to me that you're looking for problems where there aren't any? Why this interest in Arlette all of a sudden? Why now?"

"You know how you feel when you lose your keys or your wallet? You retrace your steps, you look all over, you go in circles, check out the weirdest places, and it takes a while before you say: 'Let's be logical ...' Same thing when someone dies. I have the impression that I've missed out on something ... Now can I ask you a question? Why do you always address me as *cousin*? You did it all the time in the old days too, as if you were mocking me ..."

"Mocking? Impatient, I'd say. As if I were asking, 'Are you finally going to make up your mind, cousin?'"

"Girl cousins have no idea how shy fourteen-year old boys can be. They're easily scared."

"Arlette wouldn't have seen anything, you know. If you hadn't been so embarrassed that night, you probably would have got what you wanted, in part anyway. But you'd have had to come a little closer, cousin. It wasn't up to me to make the first move. You could have just stepped up a little and we'd have been in the blind spot: from the kitchen, Arlette couldn't see anything that was going on under the carport. But you've changed the subject again, cousin."

"Not all that much. I've just come up with another reason to envy you your mother: she was always in the house, but she found a way to have blind spots ..."

"It was obvious, you know."

"What was?"

"That you envied me my mother. It wasn't me you came to see that day, it was her. And maybe that was why I didn't make the move that would have brought you closer to me."

ACCOUNTING

"Accountants are pariahs," Daniel tells me. "Untouchables. If an artist sings the blues about a businessman who'd have liked to be an artist, everybody sheds a tear. If the same singer confessed that he'd always wanted to be an accountant, people would laugh their heads off. When an accountant says that a country's on the verge of bankruptcy, he's told that he is arguing like an accountant. Imagine saying to a doctor: 'Cancer of the liver? Me? You're arguing like a medical man, Doctor ...' An accountant is by definition an idiot, a masochist, insensitive, stupid, narrow-minded, and probably neurotic — there's no doubt about it. And useless in bed, that goes without saying ... In case I've forgotten anything, I'll have you know that there's an Internet site devoted exclusively to accountant jokes. But accountants of course never visit it: how could they understand a joke?"

If I was any good at portraits, I would describe Daniel's half-smiles while he's delivering his Misunderstood Accountant monologue. I'd tell you about his winks, the little lines around his eyes when he smiles, the sparks that light up his eyes when he asks for my complicity, and you'd find him irresistible too. Daniel is looking older, like the rest of us, and while he's still a good-looking man, he doesn't have the sleek and polished looks of one of those American preachers you're instinctively wary of. His magnetism is played in a minor key: Daniel isn't a chief or a guru, he doesn't inspire admiration or fear, instead he's the one you'd like to have on your team, regardless of the sport, and win or lose, it doesn't matter — if you have to lose at least it should be with good humour. Wasn't it better to be wrong with Jean-Paul Sartre than right with Raymond Aron? And just imagine if on top of it Sartre had been handsome ...

While he has lost his baby face, Daniel still gives the impression of a man who has remained a child and has borrowed an adult's body to make himself look more credible. Comfortably ensconced behind his accountant's desk in the basement of the house in Beaurivage Gardens, he talks to me while he builds a pyramid of paper clips in their magnetic holder, as if to show me that it's all just a façade. Every time he opens his mouth, I expect that he's going to plead with me to stop pretending that I'm serious and that he's about to suggest a game of ping-pong.

But the ping-pong table disappeared long ago, as has any reference to the sixties. His office furniture is anthracite, the computer translucent, the halogen lamps high-end design, and a wide expanse of discreetly back-lit white fabric covers the entire back wall, giving the room a vaguely Japanese look. It's all intended to make us forget that we're in a basement with a low ceiling and tiny windows. No music started to play when I arrived as had happened in Sylvie's spa, but Daniel could have simply swivelled his chair to reach a sophisticated sound system and an impressive collection of CDs — among them the Beatles' *White Album*, which I recognize immediately — that he must play now and then to reward his brain between calculations. But even though he has fixed up the basement and made it comfortable, it's still a basement; what's more, it's the basement of his mother's house. All at once I understand better why Daniel's cars have always been convertibles: dear God, give me some air, give me some space! How can you spend your working life in a basement? How can you concentrate on your addition while your mother is playing solitaire in the kitchen overhead? But let's not take shortcuts, let's allow Daniel to talk about his profession. Whenever I've approached businessmen, it's been to talk about work, work, and work. The slightest reference to their private lives destabilizes them.

Why accounting? Daniel continues. First of all, because
you have to work and earn a living, that's obvious. No one
would add up figures all day long unless he's paid for it,
you know that as well as I do. It's a matter of temperament
too: you have to like numbers, rigour, precision, things done
well. When you're sixteen, you picture the accountant all
alone in his office, with no boss, and I suppose it's the
solitude and freedom that attract you. The accountant is
independent. He's also outside society, like a tennis referee.
He too watches the lines, and his logic is just as implacable:
profits in, losses out ... But I've never felt a hundred percent
like an accountant. Even if I'm well aware that every accountant says the same thing. I don't even play golf, just imagine!
In business school, my professors used to say that they could
spot us the very first day: the extroverts would become
salesmen, the introverts would become accountants. As I
was rather extroverted, they saw me in marketing or maybe
in human resources, where you need to be a slick talker and
know how to handle people, and it's true that I probably
could have made a go of it: I like people, I enjoy being
around lots of them, I like good conversation. If you know
accountants, you know there's a solidarity among them, an
esprit de corps, and that each one has his own specialty. I've
always had my network of friends and I spend a fair amount
of time on the phone consulting them, even when it would
often be simpler to find the answer by myself. I just want to
hear a voice, swap accountant jokes, listen again to the story

about the old lady who brought her bills in a shoebox every year till one fine day she made a mistake and brought in her shoes …

I've been bored in this office sometimes, I'd be a hell of a liar to deny it. Yet I've never thought about moving or changing professions. I've never felt like an accountant, but you know what life is like: you're twenty years old, you find a job you don't hate too much, you tell yourself, I'll try it out for a year or two, then we'll see — and before you know it, the boss is giving you the gold watch … Me, though, I've never had a boss, there's always that …

Did I really choose my life, or did life make the choice for me? A little of each, probably. At sixteen, I was already doing my father's taxes. I was very good at it, I think, but what I mainly know is that Arlette was immediately sure of it: right away she started promoting me. Phone calls to uncles and aunts, to Grandpa and the neighbours … In the end everybody brought in their tax forms and I bought my first calculator. The manual kind that weighs a ton and runs on elbow grease … I know it may sound weird but already at sixteen, I enjoyed filling out tax forms. It's a job that demands concentration, patience, and the ability to put up with a lot of absurdity. It's very Zen, as they say nowadays. You immerse yourself in forms, you avoid the traps and the pitfalls, you get lost, find your way again, solve the new puzzles that the tax department works hard to lay out for us every year, you turn yourself into Sherlock Holmes reading the fine print through a magnifying glass. There's even an element of suspense: will the ending be happy or unhappy, will the client have to pay or will he get a refund, will he be cheerful or morose? And soon the reward arrives. The reward is the amount you can put in the refund square, it's the ten dollar bill an uncle slips into your hand, it's the smile he gives you along with a satisfied sigh: *I thought it would be a lot more, thanks, Daniel*. The accountant and his client are accomplices, never enemies — the enemy is the government, the civil servant, the competitor. The accountant is always on the right side, always. The doctor can make a mistake, the lawyer can lose his case. But the accountant is never wrong. The columns of figures are balanced, and that's unbelievably reassuring. The accountant is an expert, his authority is undeniable. There's no room for debate, no room for doubt. And no one will ever check his calculations anyway: the client is much too happy that he doesn't have to read the forms himself ...

There's no denying, salesmen may have a better gift of the gab than accountants. They have a sense of repartee, they're droll and imaginative, they're today's *coureurs des bois*, they travel, we attribute adventures to them ... But when the time comes to cut jobs, salesmen are the first to go. At the end there'll always be an accountant in the business, even if it's just to close the books. Same thing in society: the spotlights are always trained on the singers and actors, but for every artist who goes into detox there's an accountant who goes home quietly to his house in the suburbs, turns on his TV, and watches another artist proclaiming loud and clear his contempt for bean-counters ... But can I tell you something, Benoît? The accountant may be good in math but that doesn't stop him from liking movies, going to the theatre, being moved by music. There's a right time for everything, that's all. Because they're hopeless at math, some artists assume that accountants are totally insensitive. Which proves that basically, they're even bigger bean-counters than we are: in their compartmentalized little minds, for every asset there has to be a liability ... Do you know what I do when I hear those artists spitting their contempt for accountants? I applaud. I tell them, go for it grasshopper, entertain us — we'll take care of the ants! Go go, fat ego, and don't forget to turn on your flashers when you drop your pants, to be sure that the whole world is watching ... I finally understood that there's nothing more predictable than an artist, even if they'd all sell their souls to the devil to prove the opposite. And that's precisely what is pathetic, their need for surprise, for attention, for applause ... But all this is just between us, of course. The accountants' professional association forbids us to make any official reply, it's better for business ...

When I was twenty-one, after my accounting degree, I got a job at Weston's, where I immediately started climbing the first steps that would take me to the top; up and up, as quickly as an escalator. But the sixty-hour weeks, the files I brought home, the neckties, the golf tournaments — no way!

I wanted to live, enjoy myself, be able to go around in jeans and T-shirts. And most of all, I didn't want to be forced to sell my MG because it didn't look dependable enough.

That was when Papa died. You've been there, you know how it gives you pause: you think, life is short, there must be other things to do than work your ass off ...

I handled the estate, of course. I had to meet with insurance companies, banks, the Pension Board, file the last tax return ... Actually, it was when I was filling out those forms that I decided to leave Weston's and take the plunge. Maybe I could set up an office in the basement, it would be temporary, of course, a year or two at most, I could build up a small clientele, I wouldn't have a boss, I wouldn't be required to play golf or sell my MG, and I could give Arlette a hand ...

When I was starting out, Sylvie introduced me to the network of hair salons, then to the beauticians, and since everyone has friends and relatives, I was soon turning down clients. Now I can choose. My first requirement is that I have to like the people. If I'm going to be doing their books I don't want to break into a sweat if they invite me out to eat afterwards. If I like their looks and their business is honest, I'll take them on. If not, let them find someone else. That's my personal form of fair trade. I think I made the right choice and I have no regrets, especially not about Weston's ... I've always hated the coffee-break small talk, the rumours about the boss and his secretary, the Christmas parties ... An accountant with his own office at home works hard, but he's a free man.

Arlette?

You don't have to believe me, but I never felt the slightest pressure from her. I stayed with Weston's? Fine. I set up my office in the basement of her house? Also fine. We'd reassess the situation in a year or two? Fine again. I took care of the property, did a few errands now and then, perfectly normal, in fact it gave me something else to think about. Nobody was forcing me: Arlette really wasn't demanding, and she was resourceful. She could have easily got by without me. If you take the time to look around a little, you can always find someone who'll deliver groceries or cut the grass or clean the leaves out of your eavestroughs ...

Sure I did favours for her, but it's normal to do things for your mother, right? And there were dividends: I didn't pay rent, she made me coffee, snacks ... She even had a gift for coming up with amazing topics of conversation; I still wonder where she got them ... All in all, it was a win-win situation. Now obviously a twisted mind could wonder if one of the two didn't win more than the other, but I leave questions like that to the paranoid.

Now listen, Benoît: I know what people thought. I was the right-hand man, the one who'd look after her in her old age, the good son who never left his mother, the child who never grew up, the co-dependent in Arlette's illness or who knows what — nowadays everybody's an armchair psychologist —

but why not see things as they were and not pass judgement? I had an office in the basement because it was convenient, and that's that. It suited me to have my mother available, just as it suited my mother to have a son. What's wrong with that?

I don't want to lie to you: Arlette was sick, that's a fact. But it didn't show and everyone forgot about it. Sick, Arlette? What are you talking about! For me she was a normal mother and it took a good many years before ...

Do you think that we didn't try anything? I spoke to doctors and psychologists, and they all told me the same thing: there's nothing like a behaviourist approach for curing a phobia, everybody knows that. She'd have had to go out to the carport for ten seconds, then for a minute, two minutes ... A year later, she'd have left for Kathmandu. But what can I tell you — she simply wasn't interested. Arlette was stubborn, you can't imagine how stubborn. She said *no thanks, I understand how you feel, but I don't think I need any treatment, thanks anyway.* You can't treat someone against their will, it's impossible. Should we have committed her forcibly? I'm sure you're aware of the paradox: to intern Arlette ...

So she stayed in her kitchen. Her whole life. I could hear her footsteps — counter to window, window to table, she walked very softly, Arlette, like a little mouse, she'd switch on her radio ... That's what I find hardest now — not hearing her footsteps or all the little sounds to show that a house is alive: water running through the pipes, the floor creaking, all those details ... Come with me, I want to show you something.

We go up the few steps to the kitchen. The Jell-O red countertops, the arborite table, and the vinyl-covered chairs that go *psshhh* aren't there now, which is really too bad. Daniel could have made a fortune on them with an antique dealer, where you'd never see anything from Ikea ...

Daniel opens some drawers, shows me the fridge, the stove, points out how clean it all is — but not too clean. It's a normal kitchen, where you find some crumbs in the drawers, and sesame seeds and even a little dust. Arlette wasn't a compulsive housekeeper, Daniel explains, she didn't spend all her time scrubbing and tidying. She played solitaire, she watched her birds, she copied her observations into notebooks ... If one year the thrush arrived a little earlier than usual, she'd write at once to her ornithology club. She had her regulars, her travellers, her occasional visitors, and she treated them all the way beggars used to be treated: *I'll give you some seeds, you'll give me news from warmer climates. How was Florida, Mr. Junco? Have a good trip to the Far North, dress warmly* ... Do you know how many species of birds can be seen from a window in Boucherville, Benoît? Give me a figure ...

Over seventy-five. And she knew the Latin names of all of them. You see, Benoît, that's what I find most difficult about handling the estate. It's always easy to deal with money. Utensils, dishes, clothes you distribute to the family or charities. But what do you do with a birdwatcher's life list?

Here in this drawer she kept the North American road maps that she used for following Papa's trips. She'd often

open them up at night when there was nothing good on television, and she'd invent trips for herself ... What do I do with
them now? Who would want a 1965 road map of Virginia?
Here, this was her collection of decks of cards. She knew
dozens of ways to play solitaire and she had a separate pack
for each one. Take one if you want, go ahead, as a souvenir ...

She didn't seem bored, I swear. She had her cards, her
radio, her TV programs, her telephone — even if it didn't
ring very often after your mother died ... And she'd read two
or three books a week, fat novels that her friend Laurette
brought her from the library. She'd tell me about them sometimes: they were always stories of grand passions set during
the American Civil War, or under the Occupation, or during
the Russian Revolution, and from all her reading she knew a
lot more history than I did, I guarantee ... She had a whole
network of women friends: Laurette, who lived at the corner
of the street, with whom she'd talk about books for hours;
Odile, another neighbour who often dropped in and would
have loved to take her to the Boucherville Islands; and all the
other women I didn't know, who'd drop in for tea or chat on
the phone ...

She was a very keen recycler, Daniel went on, opening a
drawer and taking out jars full of rubber bands, plastic ties,
metal strips from cans. "What will I do with all this, can you
tell me? What can you do with things that are left that you
can't give away?"

I look at the plastic ties and the rubber bands, and it feels as if I'm visiting a museum devoted to the housewife, the domestic world — and why not quite simply to *domestic science*, along with all the other sciences.

Daniel keeps looking at the jars full of ties from bags of milk, coughing slightly to conceal his emotion, while I go to the window and look at the maple tree, a maple so close and yet so far. I remember what Jocelyne said about air-traffic controllers, and I switch metaphors: Arlette in her control tower observing the birds and feeding them ... When do pilots most need the controller? During take off or landing? Do the controllers use binoculars, like Arlette? And if so, what is their range?

"What are you going to do now?"

"Sell the house," Daniel replies, after another slight cough. "There's nothing to keep me here now. A colleague suggested that we share an office near my place. He's an old friend and we get along well. I'll have a real office, with a secretary, for the first time in my life ... I want to try it out for a year or two, then we'll see ... I know, I've said that before, but that's it, what can I tell you ... I could also fix up an office at home, there's enough room, but I've always preferred to have my office in another place. It's best to have solid walls between your public life and your private life."

"Private life?"

"Surely you don't think I've spent my whole life under my mother's skirts, do you?"

I'd like to tell him, "Of course not," even though it's what

I've always thought, but he doesn't give me time.

"There's another thing you should know about account-ants: they're very discreet."

⚗

One day Jocelyne told me about a study showing that most couples reproduce their parents' marriage. The children of divorced parents divorce more often than most, while those whose parents had a happy marriage enter confidently into marriage and therefore have better chances of success. And that was where I expected to find my cousins: I expected fearful loves, stunted, neurotic, musty-smelling loves, plas-tic loves that split open at the first cold snap ... Instead, they've both told me about simple, happy love stories, the kind we wish for our best friends. Sylvie and Daniel are both discreet and stable, and so are their love stories.

LOVE STORY, TAKE ONE

He came in for a haircut, Sylvie tells me. He came in for a haircut, he looked a little lost, and right away I knew he was the one.

Sylvie is obviously thrilled to talk about her Jean-Claude. She smiles, relaxes, and now she's disarmed, defenceless, as if she were on vacation.

It was back when I was working with Madame Patenaude, she says, slowly putting her coffee cup on the desk. She had a salon just across the street, you could see where it was if you crane your neck, but it's not worth the trouble, it was a salon like any other, and it's been sold now ... I was twenty-two and I hadn't known many men. Not out of scruples, I was no Little Miss Prig, I had hormones like everybody else, it's just that I hadn't found what I was looking for. Sometimes two or three of us girls would go out together, we'd get dressed to kill and go to a disco, and you'd better believe me, there was plenty of buzz around us; I felt like a flower in the middle of a field, I just had to stand there, let myself sway in the breeze, and along came the bees. The guys talked, told me about their exploits, let their motors run, and I didn't stop them. They tried so hard to impress me, so I'd let them win me over out of pity, you know, like when you buy something from a salesman because he's put on a good show. You buy his stuff, but then you don't know what to do with it, so it ends up in a closet or at a garage sale ... The first time, it was always fine, even exciting, all new and bright and shiny, but the second time would be deadly: they'd talk about the same exploits in the same way, word for word, they revved up the same motor ... Already they were starting to repeat themselves, you know what I mean? I'd want to tell them, *Listen, man, find something else, okay, or rather, don't try, nothing says you have to impress me ...*

Jean-Claude didn't try to impress me, didn't try to make me feel sorry for him either — that type was easy to spot — he was just ... he was just a little lost, that's all. He walked into the salon, it was lunchtime, he told us his truck was being fixed at the garage across the street and he'd decided to get his hair fixed while he waited for the truck, if you've got the time, that is ...

I told him that we might have the time, but it could be a

bit complicated, since we were hairdressers for women and we were forbidden by law to *fix* men's hair ... You should have seen the look on him! As if he'd stuck his finger in an electrical outlet: he turned beet red, looked all around, he didn't know what to do with himself, I don't think he'd have been any more embarrassed if he'd accidentally gone into a women's washroom.

He tried to apologize, but he kept getting so tangled up in his words that I couldn't help laughing. I told him, *don't worry, you aren't the first, anyone can make a mistake*, he finally realized he hadn't committed any crime, then he apologized again, and eventually he left. Which could be the end of the story, but just before he left, I told him *see you next time* ... The words came out just like that. Can you believe it? I'd only seen him for two minutes, and during those two minutes all he did was apologize, and there I am asking him to come back ... For the first time in my life, it was me who'd made the first move and I didn't even realize it.

"Seems to me the lettering's big enough," Madame Patenaude said as she watched him cross the street. "Makes you wonder if some people know how to read."

I was totally stunned. Lettering? What lettering?

"In the window," Madame Patenaude pointed out, sounding exasperated. "WOMEN'S HAIRSTYLISTS ... Don't tell me you've never noticed either. How long've you been working here anyway?"

"Maybe his mind was somewhere else."

"Oh, it was somewhere else all right, in the clouds if you ask me! A normal person wouldn't make a mistake like that!"

She kept griping and I kept quiet. It was her way of showing that she was smarter than anyone else, I was used to it. Since I already knew all her tunes by heart I pretended to listen, but I was daydreaming. Needless to say there wasn't a chance in a thousand that he'd come back. He'd been in the neighbourhood by accident, he hadn't even said his name ... All I knew was that he worked for a courier service — he had on a uniform — but I couldn't even remember which one. I didn't know a thing about him but I hoped he'd be back, I hoped so much it scared me. I already knew that he was the one. Can you believe it?

Three days later, he walks into the salon on the stroke of noon, holding a fat envelope. He shows me the address, written in big letters with a felt pen: a chemical company in an industrial park in Laval. He tells me he got lost along the way, asks if I could show him where it is ... I pretend to explain to him that we're in Boucherville, on the south shore of Montreal, and that Laval is north of the city, but I know perfectly well that he already knows and that he knows that I know, it's just a way of getting acquainted; he pretends he's listening but his eyes are saying something else, mine too, I don't think I've ever smiled so much in my entire life, my cheeks ache, and while I talk I try to pick up as much information as possible, I look at his hair, his fingers, his nails, I record the sound of his voice, it takes maybe two minutes, but it's amazing what you can find out in two minutes, if our brains always worked that fast we'd learn Chinese in two hours ... So he leaves, muttering some apology that I don't listen to: the only thing that interests me is his smile.

"Some messenger!" says Madame Patenaude when the door shuts behind him. "Doesn't know the difference between Laval and Boucherville! They aren't too fussy who they hire nowadays! What kind of ignoramus do you think I am? But as they say, it takes all kinds ..."

She concluded her brilliant philosophical lecture with a huge exasperated sigh but you could tell that she was rather proud of herself: Madame Patenaude wasn't the kind of person who'd confuse Laval and Boucherville, no sir, she was much too intelligent!

He came back the next day — again at noon. He didn't have a letter or a package or anything, just his empty hands and his smile. He told me he didn't know how to dance, I told him it didn't matter; he told me *I'd like to take you out to* eat, I said *all right, as long as we eat together*; he said *fine with me, as long as it's anywhere at all*. And that was it.

"He moves fast!" says Madame Patenaude when he's gone.

"Not really," I say, and Madame Patenaude gives me a strange look.

I think it was the first time I hadn't pretended to agree with her and she wasn't sure how to react.

Six months later, we moved in together. At first we were happy with an ordinary little apartment. I'd already been thinking about opening my spa and Jean-Claude was always on the road, so we didn't want the burden of a house. Also, I'd never been crazy about gardening ...

I couldn't imagine myself with anyone but him — no way, impossible. He's not a man who'll get down on his knees and recite poetry, or walk on his hands to make me laugh, he's just ... he's just a good guy: quiet, considerate, kind ... We've been together nearly thirty years now and I've never felt that he was repeating himself. Every night, he's got something new to tell me, something he saw on the road, a joke he heard on the radio, just anecdotes, you know, bits of conversation he picked up at a client's, anything at all — but he can always find stories I'll be interested in, and I'm the one he wants to tell them to ... Jean-Claude is a really good guy. Mama liked him a lot.

No, we aren't married. I know what we've got, I trust him, and a piece of paper with a signature on it won't ... Nobody's obliged to get married nowadays, right? What about you, are you married?

We all make our own choices ... I'd be lying if I said we'd never thought of it. Jean-Claude would've liked it: he's from a traditional family, he's fairly traditional himself, I think he'd have liked that. But there was Arlette, you understand? Just imagine: the white gown, the organ, the confetti, the reception. Arlette's daughter is getting married, but the bride's mother stays home ...

That may not be the main reason, no, I wouldn't say that. But I'd be lying if I said that it wasn't a factor.

Children? I'd have liked children, so would he. But I had to get established first. People like you, at a university, you've got paid holidays and job security, and you can pick up again when you want, but for us in the private sector, it's not so simple, we work hard to build up a clientele ...

And then the time went by. After thirty, it's as if the clocks are on speed, especially the biological clock ... We tried as much as we could, but it's not something you can order, it's not enough to want it, and then the more time passed, the harder it became ... We tried for three years, then we decided to cross it off our list. Sure, we could have tried other ways, but all that business with test-tubes and drugs, no thanks. A baby, for me, grows in a womb, not a lab. We could have adopted, we took the first steps, but there's a waiting list, you have to fill out forms, meet with social workers who want to know why you want a child and you don't know what to tell them, you feel as if you're back in school, writing an exam you haven't studied for. Why do I want a child? What a weird question! Do I ask you why you breathe, Ms. Social Worker? In the end we said *no thanks, not for us.* We tried to get over it and we spent time with our nieces and nephews, luckily we have lots ... And you know what, cousin? There's this strange idea that's been running through my head for a while now, and I'd like to talk it over with you, you'll tell me what you think.

I'm fifty now, you see, and I'm getting tired, like every-body else. The house is paid for, I've got savings, I could easily sell my business and enjoy life a little, just enjoy life, travel with Jean-Claude, take a real break, watch TV, walk, nothing fancy ... I'm giving myself another five years max, maybe not even that. The trouble is, I don't want to sell to just anybody. I'm attached to this business, you see, it may not be much but I built it myself, it's my creation in a way, and I don't want it to end up in the wrong hands ... The simplest thing would be to work like a maniac for a year or so to inflate the turnover, then sell for a good price, and so long, it's been swell. But I've got another idea. I've got an employee I like a lot — Julie. She's serious, hard-working, conscientious, she always wants to learn, and it's a pleasure to watch her. She doesn't know yet, but she's the one I want to leave it to. I'm prepared to let her have it for a lower price, that doesn't bother me, I'm even prepared to finance her and I'd be happy if she was the one taking over, I'm sure she'd be up to it ... In a way it's as if I were choosing my daughter, isn't it? What do you think?

True, you aren't a psychologist, but I'm not asking for psychological advice or a professor's advice, just your advice as a cousin. It's a good idea, don't you think?

Really? I'm very glad you think so too.

Now then, can I ask you one last thing, cousin? At the funeral parlour, when the priest was saying his prayers — or rather, while he was trying to get around his Alzheimer's — I thought, hey, I could get married now, treat myself to a beautiful church wedding, it would be strange though, after living together for thirty years, an old-fashioned marriage with a white gown ... I haven't talked with Jean-Claude about it. I'd be too afraid it would bring bad luck. But if he brings it up, if it's important to him, then we'll see.

LOVE STORY, TAKE TWO

J've always enjoyed charming people, Daniel tells me. Which was a good thing, because I had what it took. I was twenty years old with all my teeth, and I realized the effect I had on girls. I never had to work at it too hard — just enough for it to be exciting — and I took advantage of it. What I liked best was the first time, the very first time, when I'd go up to the girl and smell all her perfumes at the same time, *oh boy*, every time I felt like saying, Thank you, God, for inventing life. Yes, I took advantage of it, but I always told them the truth, I always put my cards on the table: I'm twenty years old and I want to be twenty for a long time; if you want to complicate your life, I'm not your man, look elsewhere, serious girls please abstain. They'd say *yes, all right, I know what I'm getting into*. Often they really thought so, which was fine with me; but sometimes they didn't and oh oh, problem time. Sure, it's wonderful, the excitement of the first days, but afterwards it's another story. And don't forget, I'm just a little accountant: I can't feel any emotion whatsoever, everybody knows that, so handling the break-ups ...

And then one day I was twenty-five, and I thought I'd seen it all. I wanted something more serious, I felt like settling down, making an accountant of myself ...

And that's when I met Marie. The problem with her was that the roles were reversed: she didn't want a stable relationship. If she was attracted to me at first, it was precisely because I had a reputation for not being serious. Now, I have to say Marie was getting over something complicated: she'd just been divorced, she had two little girls, her ex was possessive — the kind who makes threats, and also the kind who carries them out, really sick, so she just wanted me now and then, to take her mind off her problems, but that was all.

For six months I made myself very small, very obliging. We only saw each other now and then, we had an understanding, once a week maybe, sometimes not even that. She'd call when she could free herself, we'd go out to eat or to a movie, then she'd spend an hour or two at my place, and I'd take her home as soon as possible so she could let the sitter go. Sometimes too we'd go out *en famille*, if I can put it that way, which was just fine with me: we'd take the girls to La Ronde or the pool, eat barbecued chicken at Saint-Hubert, and sometimes Marie would let me slip into her bed, when we were very sure that the girls were fast asleep; we'd caress one another in silence, ears pricked, minds vaguely elsewhere, but it was still good, I'd take what I could, even if it was very little ...

I was ready for a more serious commitment, but I played along anyway. I was the person she wanted me to be and I found myself spending evenings at home, trying to hypnotize the phone to make it ring ... I could hardly recognize myself, but at the same time I didn't mind. I couldn't see Marie as often as I'd have liked, but whenever I did it was a feast. Besides, there was the illicit, even dangerous side to it: her ex-husband was well-known in political circles and you never know who those people hang out with ... It may sound ridiculous, but it added spice.

I was happy just to be available, to make myself very small, very slight; I told myself that eventually I'd domesticate her and that she'd realize I wasn't as superficial as she thought. I was patient, I did little things for her just to be together, but the more little things I did for her, the more I wanted to be with her, and the more I felt like a prisoner of my beautiful jailor, as it says in the song. Besides, there were the girls ...

Two little girls, aged one and three. Two little bundles of curls with big eyes in the middle. Two little girls who were even better than their mother at winning you over, and that was something. I just wanted to tell them stories, make them laugh, and when they put their little hands in mine, when they fell asleep over my shoulder, when they looked at me with their big eyes, they were irresistible, that's the only word; I felt wobbly inside my head … Back home, I'd try to glue the pieces together as best I could, but I already knew I'd never be the same. I didn't feel like watching TV or playing tennis any more — and even less like going to a bar. All I wanted was to take the girls to the playground and become for them the Superman who could throw a stone across the river, the doctor who could pull out a splinter, the one who knew everything. I tell you, Benoît, I was hooked — and hooked bad.

And now, picture this: it's Saturday afternoon and I'm at Marie's. While she's bathing Maude — she's the younger — I'm folding the clothes as they come out of the dryer. Of all the household tasks on this earth, that one has always been my favourite: clothes that are nice and warm, that smell good, summer dresses the size of a handkerchief, little shirts with baby elephants, you can't get over how small they are … All of a sudden, there he is. The ex. The violent husband. I'd imagined a muscleman, you see, some big hulk, but not at all, he's more like a little weasel, he's a good head shorter than me but that doesn't stop him from clenching his fists and looking me up and down. He reeks of booze and doesn't look all that solid on his feet, which gives me another advantage. I doubt that we'll fight — he's not the kind who'd take on someone stronger, especially in front of his daughters — but you never know what goes on inside a cracked head …

"Who the hell are you?" he asks.

Before I can say a word, Marie steps in between us.

"Daniel, this is Michel. Michel, this is Daniel."

She tries to speak as neutrally as possible, but I can barely recognize her voice, it's so dry. Michel goes on staring at me, with such contempt his eyes look yellow. I hold out my hand, he ignores it.

"Who is he?" he grunts at Marie, never taking his eyes off me.

"My accountant," she says.

Which is the truth, of course, but I'm disappointed when she introduces me like that, terribly disappointed, you can't imagine — especially because Michel unclenches his fists and sends me a condescending smile: after all, he's not going to be scared of an accountant! But before he's finished unclenching them, Marie speaks up again.

"He's also my lover," she says. "We … We're going to get married."

Michel goes rigid. He takes a step towards me and stands there just under my nose; he keeps staring, but I don't budge, I wait for him to make the first move, while doing nothing that might provoke him. He gives me a scowl that's the equivalent of spitting in my face, but I don't react. Finally, he turns and leaves, slamming the door; he slams his car door just as hard, starts it, making the tires squeal, and that's it. No brawl, no violence, but it will take us a good hour to eliminate our excess adrenaline — I don't know how that poison works exactly, but I have the impression that you never get rid of it altogether, that it settles somewhere in your bones ... Just talking about it I can feel it starting to circulate in my veins again ...

That was the last time we saw him. Exit ex. He was still around, but only every other weekend. He was an on-and-off father, who sent cheques intermittently. I thank him all the same: it's because of him, after all, that Marie asked me to marry her.

I waited a while before bringing up the subject again. One day when we were in bed together, I mentioned her proposal. She didn't ask what proposal, she knew what I was talking about right away.

And that's the story, Benoît. That's how I became a faithful husband and a non-practising lady's man. ... I've never regretted it for one second. The girls are grown up, they're adults now — I'm sure you saw them at the funeral parlour, it's hard not to notice them.

And now, I imagine, you're going to ask what our wedding was like.

Don't play innocent, I can see you coming, with your questions ... No, Arlette wasn't there. Sylvie was my witness, Marie invited her best friend, the two girls were maids of honour, and that was that. It couldn't have been more simple. Ten minutes at the court house and that was it. After that we went to Arlette's, who'd prepared our wedding feast.

She was happy, you can't imagine how happy. She showered gifts on the girls, made them doll's clothes. The kind of grandma who spoils you rotten. She often invited us for Sunday supper ...

I didn't feel like shouting from the rooftops that we were married, I never wanted to shout anything from the rooftops at all, for that matter, heights make me dizzy. You have to understand that I'm really not an artist ... It was just the way things worked out that our relationship started off so discreetly, but it was by choice that it continued that way. My clients, my friends — nobody knew I was married. Maybe some people think I'm still living at my mother's, like a teenager who doesn't want to grow up, others probably think I'm gay, but since nobody asks me directly, I don't have to deny anything. People always think what they want to anyway ... *Let it be*, man. By the way, I imagine you've got the Beatles anthology, I know you. You were so crazy about George, you must love the acoustic version of "While My Guitar," right? In my opinion, it's better than the version on the *White Album*. It's as if George is right there in your living room, he takes his guitar out of its case, says *listen, I've just composed something, I don't know if it's any good, listen up ...*

Daniel slides the CD into the player, finds the track, and George tells us very softly that he sees the love that's sleeping ...

I listen to him, thinking that both Daniel and Sylvie are as discreet in love as in life, and they know how lucky they are. Psychologists, please abstain.

And now it's time for me to withdraw, on tiptoe.

MADAME AND MANAGEMENT, MONSIEUR AND HOUSEWORK

 I don't mind doing housework. Laundry in particular I quite enjoy. If you've got nothing else to do, of course, it's just one trivial chore among others, but if you wait for the right moment — when you have an article to write or a lecture to prepare, for instance — the chore is a godsend. Laundry isn't about dirty linen, it's about mood. Arlette would agree, of that I'm sure.

Choosing the cycle, adding the soap, filling the machine, closing the lid, there we go, now I can settle in at my computer, my next break has already been programmed: in less than an hour I'll have to transfer the clothes to the dryer, and I'll enjoy a pause that's not only legitimate but also useful. *Monsieur* is efficient. As efficient as the housewife who knows sound management principles. As it happens, the title of my article is "Madame et Management." Housework is the administration of domestic matters, according to the dictionary. Why shouldn't it be studied in business school? Doing housework means looking after the house, creating harmony. Doing housework means looking after your business, whatever it is, and there's no such thing as a small business, as I often tell my students, any more than there's a small profit or small happiness.

I always try to destabilize my M.A. students by sending them into the field to observe organizations that are not multinationals or government departments. I insist that they study very small businesses, whose organization charts are sometimes family trees — Chinese restaurants, convenience stores, florists — and even smaller ones: the accountant who works at home, the watchmaker, the man who puts up clotheslines, the one who roots around in the garbage for recyclable cans the day after national holidays. All have to manage information so as to make effective decisions, so there must be a way to study objectively their behaviour and to learn something from it. We hope that the can recycler won't have to fight the competition to determine his route, and it's hard to imagine him hiring a lawyer to defend his rights ... In such cases, how is the competition governed?

I have just realized that I've been teaching for more than twenty years but have never thought to ask my students to observe that unit of consumption, which is what the economists call households. Look at your parents: who is responsible for the garbage and recycling, who does the ironing, who is Minister of External Affairs? If Arlette were still alive, I'd ask her permission to set up cameras in her house: to observe her movements when she's cleaning the sink or the washbasin, washing the bathroom curtains, ironing shirts ... To the student in too big a hurry to study how Bombardier or the Bank of Montreal operates, I would talk about housework as an invariable production cell, a modest and necessary activity that's performed far from the grand principles and social debates, which makes it one of the great historical constants ... A colleague pointed out one day that the infantry units of every modern army always include about ten soldiers, twelve at most. The same was true for the Roman army and the armies of Genghis Khan, Napoleon, and Hitler ... Whatever the language, the country, or the degree of technological development, it seems that ten or twelve is the optimal number for engaging in an effective warlike activity — or for playing football, selecting a jury, founding a religion ... I like constants like that. As in mathematics, they make it easier for us to think. Housework is the constant of constants: what can we draw from that?

I empty the washing machine absent-mindedly while think-ing about my article, I program the dryer to give me a break in forty minutes, and I rush back up to my office ... *house-hold, management, managing housework to manage oneself* ... a rich etymology.

I make a few more notes, and I'm startled when the dryer

buzzer goes off. Now comes the best moment, I agree with you, Daniel: folding laundry that's still warm, that has the lovely scent of a chemical product called *Country Morning* (marketing specialists have obviously never set foot in the country, but I like their notion of what it's like) ... Make neat piles, arrange things in order ... Folding clothes is treating yourself to a warm game of solitaire. Black queen on red king, wool sock on wool sock ...

What my mother liked best was ironing. She'd always wait till we came home from school to start, as if she wanted us to see her mastery of the steam iron. She never gave me ironing lessons — it was a job for girls — but I learned anyway, by observing her. Start on the side with the buttons, which will nestle in the groove in the sole plate of the iron, next do the back, then the buttonhole placket, on to the sleeves, and finally the collar, which I always keep for the end ... You have to iron at least three shirts before the iron reaches the right temperature, then you can let yourself be carried away by the pleasant languor that routine allows. The iron glides over the cloth, and there goes your head on a journey.

Once my mother had finished ironing a shirt, she'd hold it up in front of her to examine it carefully.

I would see her then with furrowed brow, searching for a crease she'd overlooked, then she'd give a faint smile of satisfaction when she didn't find any. After that, she would fold the shirt carefully, which must have frustrated her just a bit, but closets were tiny back then and she couldn't exhibit her works permanently on their hangers ...

Why did she wait till we were home to do her ironing? Because, quite simply, ironing is the final step: it's normal to do it at the end of the day ... Maybe. But I still believe that she was putting on a show: she seemed to like our being there around the ironing board, and she'd lay it on a bit thick when she sensed we were paying attention, turning the shirt over with a broader movement and producing some bursts of steam, why not? it's always impressive ...

Cécile enjoyed ironing. Maybe it was the thought of renewal that pleased her, or maybe she was delighted that finally she'd finished the laundry, a chore that lasted all day Monday, or maybe she was quite simply happy that we were admiring her work. All of the above, none of the above? I'll never know, just as I'll never be able to master the art of pressing with a damp cloth: the soaking wet cloth, the hot iron spitting steam, like the spacecraft on *Star Trek* ... Even now, when I'm ironing my shirts, I'll sometimes produce some extra bursts of steam just for the pleasure of creating my own special effects.

Housework is a secret passage that lets you go back as often as you want to the kitchen of your childhood, like the secret passage in Clue that led from the kitchen to the living room if I remember correctly, or maybe it was the library ...

(*He's off again, whispers Patricia, there he goes ...*)

The idea of a secret passage strikes me as powerful, but I don't quite see how I can work it into an article for a management journal ...

Now why don't I treat myself to a game of solitaire? I'm on sabbatical, after all. A cold game of solitaire between the warm piles of clothes, a game in the middle of the afternoon — supreme luxury — and with a deck of Arlette's cards ...

I clear a space for myself between two piles of towels and I lay out the cards on the table.

I place my red six on the black seven, thereby making room for my king of clubs, which allows me to turn over another card, let's hope it's a red eight ...

I've always been an avid player of solitaire, of the real thing. Don't talk to me about those programs installed in our computers that only wear out the screens prematurely. The game was supposed to teach us patience — which is the British name for it — but instead it encourages us to pro-crastinate: one more hand and I'll get to work on my article, just one, I promise ... I prefer real cards, good old cards that are creased and worn from handling, that you can cheat with honestly. (Did you cheat now and then, Arlette, or were you too perfect to do that?)

It's an urge that comes over me in spurts. For a few days I'll play compulsively, then I'll tire of it. I began as a child, when I was in a cast after a hockey accident; I kept it up during my teenage years, but only on the eve of exams. When you don't have anything to do there's nothing more boring than solitaire. But if you're studying for a math exam and want to steal some time from your studies — sheer delight! (What exam were you studying for all your life, Arlette?)

I went through another phase in my thirties, when I taught my children the game. It was as good a way as any to teach them numbers and colours, perseverance, expectation, surprise: you place your ace of hearts at the top, you see, which gives you the chance to finally open the hidden pack of cards, and who knows what you'll find there? Another ace, maybe, or else a map that will take us to a hidden treasure ... My children soon moved on to Pacman and intergalactic battles, as did I for that matter, but I always came back to good old solitaire, played with real cards. My last attack goes back around ten years, when I stopped smoking and was searching desperately for something to do with my hands. Black eight on red nine, no, I won't go out and buy cigarettes and I won't try to smoke my seven of clubs either. I turn over three more cards ... Thank you, solitaire, it's because of you that it wasn't as hard to break the habit as it could have been. True, I may have exchanged one habit for another, but this one's innocuous, and you wouldn't contradict me, Arlette: is there any game as innocuous as solitaire, is there anyone on earth who's more harmless than Arlette playing solitaire? I'm sure the great Zen masters play it too: black six on red seven, nothing like it for meditating, for taking your mind off something, for cheering yourself up. There are days when the quickest hands of solitaire are welcome. And while putting the cards in order, you can sometimes put order into your thoughts as well, especially the ones that resist order.

Has anyone ever thought of using solitaire to communicate with spirits? Let's give it a try, just to see: eight of clubs, jack of spades, what are you thinking about, Arlette, in your red and white kitchen, while you lay out your cards on the table in neat little piles? You look at the eight of hearts, then you notice a crumb of bread left behind on the table, the last vestige of the snack you served Daniel before he left to see a client. Will you get up and remove that crumb or go on playing? There you are, off in the clouds, Arlette — me too, for that matter. The kitchen is a maze, like fractals that decompose to infinity yet remain always the same. You get up and take a damp rag, you wipe the table, you rinse the rag to prevent mildew, you look out the window for a minute: it's cold and damp outside, the air is saturated with a fine icy mist, you were right to advise Daniel to wear his overcoat, in fact the weatherman Alcide Ouellette urged his listeners to bundle up this morning, the other meteorologists are often wrong, but Alcide …

You always listen to the weather forecast, Arlette, you always know what it's like outside for others, but what is it like for you? You've never had a sunburn, never felt rain falling on your head, heard the snow grind its teeth, felt the bite of cold on your skin. Outside, it's raining, it's cold. It's the first of November in no matter what year, but for you it makes no difference. You wipe off the table, you sit down again, you turn over three cards: two of spades, two of spades, what on earth are you going to do with that two of spades?

Sometimes you win, sometimes not. There's nothing disastrous about losing, winning barely puts a satisfied smile on your face. You get up, you look out the window, maybe you go to your sewing machine to make uniforms for the majorettes while you wait for Cécile to call ... Be careful if you go out, Cécile, the roads are liable to be slippery, they said so on the radio this morning ...

Idiotic questions: Do you have boots and a coat, Arlette? Do you have an umbrella, a raincoat, a hat? What use would they be to you?

You come back to the kitchen table, turn over the cards, think about your children — they're so devoted, so close to you. Sylvie and Daniel don't seem to have suffered too much from your illness, they seem as well-balanced as anyone else, more than a fair number of my colleagues even. If you inoculated them with the fear virus, you certainly didn't give them too strong a dose ...

Businessmen always react the same way when you ask how their business is doing: never do they boast about stupendous results, for fear of stirring up the competition, but they never admit that things are going badly either, even if it's common knowledge that they're on the verge of bankruptcy. They stick with the vague. Compromise themselves as little as possible. Their business is always doing *fine*, no more than that. I'd be willing to bet that most psychologists' clients have the same kind of reflex when they allude to their past: "I don't understand, I had a normal childhood, in a normal family …" Ask them a few more questions and they'll soon confess that their father was a pathological gambler and their mother a junkie and a hooker, but they'll still repeat that it was a normal childhood, in a normal family. They've had just one family and it was that one. How could it *not* be normal? Some families are normally pathological, others are normally dysfunctional, normally neurotic, normally normal …

May I speak frankly, Arlette? You did after all oblige your children to take care of you, right? Nicely, I grant you that, but it doesn't change anything.

They don't seem unhappy, that too I grant you. They've even been quite successful, if you want my opinion. And perhaps that's what I find hardest to swallow … You make clothes for Sylvie, she gives you permanents; Daniel does your shopping, you make him snacks … Fair's fair. Give and receive. It seems so simple, so natural. I've never been able to give my mother a thing: either the gift was not appropriate or she made us feel that it wasn't our role to give her something, or else she pretended to accept it and then gave it back the next day, with compound interest. If someone doesn't know how to receive, can he truly give?

Cécile called you every day, Arlette. Every day. She bought parts for your sewing machine, thread, fabric, bird-seed, she scoured the city to be of service to you … Did you too have the impression that you could never give her anything, Arlette? What was it like to have Cécile for a sister?

What would you say if you could speak to me, you who had such a long conversation with her?

RED FIVE ON BLACK SIX

You're a know-it-all now and then, Aunt Arlette tells me, but you've managed to surprise me anyway. I thought that university professors didn't know how to listen. Which just goes to show you, people can always make mistakes, as much here as anywhere else ... I liked the fact that you got my children to talk, that you knew how to step aside. You added some remarks of your own, which is normal, but I still felt as if I were hearing their voices. Now that I know you can hear me, I'd like you to open your ears and not try to interrupt. There's just a tiny bit of energy left in my old batteries and I don't know how long they'll hold out. I won't be able to repeat things or explain things for very long, so try listening to what I say instead of how I say it: I didn't go to school as long as you did, but I still managed to learn a fair amount when I was alive. If I'd gone to school longer I imagine I'd have learned how to put together fine, elegant sentences, maybe sentences are like music, maybe there are rules to respect about rhythm and tempo and all that, but there's no reason why we can't speak even if we don't know all the rules, I sometimes even think we're better off not knowing them, it's like the Beatles, who my children were so crazy about, at first they didn't know much about music theory, those Beatles, but that didn't stop them from strumming away on their guitars and inventing melodies that nobody'd ever heard, and since they didn't know the rules, they didn't even know they were breaking them, yet the fact remains that we still sing those songs of theirs, but I don't want to get tangled up in my thoughts too much, I just wanted to tell you to listen properly, even if my sentences are strange, and if you have trouble understanding, ask Patricia to help you, she knows all about translation, she's a good little girl, Patricia, it was a smart move, marrying her, I'm telling you that right away before I forget, and you'll thank her for making a little room for me next to her, she was very sweet.

I'd like to tell you that I didn't really choose my life, Benoît. I didn't choose my life and I certainly didn't choose my illness. Not that I have any regrets, no, I'd be very ungrateful if I had to regret anything at all, it's just that the film had started long before we got to the theatre, we look at the characters and wonder how they always know what to say and what to do and where to go, it's as if they know all the lines in advance, so we make ourselves very small, we observe, we try to find our place, and it takes time before we realize that we're not just spectators, that we've got something to say, that we can even change the story if we want, often we only realize it when the film is half over, but I've never really understood that. If we don't jump on the train when we're very small, all we can do is stand there and watch it go by. But how do you jump on a train when it's already going so fast?

Even if the train had stopped, even if the doors were wide open, I was so small that I couldn't climb on board. I'd have needed strong arms, muscular arms, like a father's, to lift me up as if it were nothing, upsadaisy, with a little help it's child's play, here we are on the train and we didn't even realize it, but I didn't have a father, that was the problem, I didn't have a father. When I try to find a beginning, that's where I always balk.

My mother used to say that there'd been a great war over there in the old countries, and that during it my father had died, and they'd never found his body, *and we have to pray for him, young lady, maybe the good Lord will find him, now eat your soup*. Some people have a gift for stopping blood, my mother's gift was for changing the subject. I think it's hereditary.

Children sometimes misunderstand, but they hear everything. I always knew that my mother's story was a pack of lies. If my father had died in the war, then he was a hero, and when you've got a hero in the family, you talk about him all the time, you show photos, you tell stories, you create legends that you end up actually believing — but you don't try to change the subject. A hero no one talks about is pointless, it's as if he had squandered his life twice.

His name was never spoken at home, but you should have heard the concert of murmurs in the lanes and in the schoolyard and at my girlfriends' houses; people forget how well a child's ears work. Now and then they'd say that someone had heard from someone else that my father was living in the States and that he sometimes came back to Montreal, and as a matter of fact that same someone's sister-in-law worked at the post office and she could swear that Mama received a parcel from the States every month, and that in the package were clothes of a kind that you never saw anyone wearing around here, *and don't the Desmarais girls dress well? I'm not saying that to run them down, it's just that I wonder, and I'm not the only one, do the rest of you think it's normal for fatherless girls to have such pretty dresses* ... Another one had a sister-in-law or a cousin who worked at the bank and who could swear that every month, Madame Desmarais got a cheque from the States, *I can't say for how much, that would be indiscreet and you know that's not like me, but still I can tell you that if it was me I wouldn't be complaining all the time if I had that kind of money* ...

They whispered, but I could hear it all, I was like the bionic woman on TV, I don't know if you remember Lindsay Wagner, my ears were bionic and I couldn't lower the volume, I'd be walking in the lane and I'd hear conversations, I'd go to my friends' houses to play and I could hear what their mothers told them before I'd even stepped inside the house, before I'd knocked on the door; as soon as I walked in I'd hear silence fall, but as soon as I started to play, the buzzing would start up again, like on the telephone when the lines are crossed and you can hear distant voices, *and if that's not enough, apparently he was never a soldier, I got that from my brother-in-law who really did fight in the war, anyway if he'd died in the war she would have got a war widow's pension ...*

I never did know the truth, let me tell you that right away, I never knew if my father was dead or alive, if the cheques came from the States or from the Department of Veterans' Affairs; it would have been easy to find out, I'd have just had to pick up the phone, I've always been good at getting what I wanted on the phone, and I had the patience needed to get information from government departments, I could have figured out how to get the information, but I never did. My mother had taught me how to change the subject. If a thing wasn't talked about, it didn't exist. When you're used to something and you've figured out some other way to sort things out, it's no use taking the trouble to find out. Maybe some day I'll go walking in other rooms than the one I'm in now, maybe I'll find a Bureau of Unresolved Questions at the end of a corridor, I'll just have to push open the door and take a number, but why bother? One thing that you lose quickly up here is curiosity. It's hard to explain why, it's as if time doesn't pass in the same way, as if we no longer understand why the seconds should always follow one another in the same order — from left to right, one after another — and if there's no longer a reason for questions to come before answers, then there's no reason to look for the right word to express what you want; at first it seems very strange but you get used to it, you'll find that out soon enough, you'll make pyramids of seconds, then you'll watch them collapse in silence, the way I do, and then you'll do the same thing with words.

I've never known the truth, but the real story isn't what matters. What matters are the words I heard, the ones that entered my head when I was a little girl, and even if I didn't understand every one of them, I could always sense their flavour, their coating, I knew that they tasted of nastiness; to avoid hearing them I'd have had to use earplugs, and even that wouldn't have been enough, I'd have seen the looks on those who talked behind my back, so to avoid seeing them I'd have had to wear blinkers and always walk with my eyes to the ground, but even blind I'd have been able to sense their remarks circling above my head like black birds, so as you can see, there was really no solution.

The three or four doctors I saw told me I had an illness, they claimed I'd have to be desensitized little by little, as with allergies, they said I'd have to overcome my anxiety, tame the monsters, they expected me to make my fears jump through rings of fire like in the circus, but there were no monsters, no wild beasts, it was just that I heard everything, do you understand? I heard too much, like the bionic woman. Imagine that you switch on the radio and you hear all the stations at once.

The solution would be to switch it off, but you can't stop people from talking or thinking, so the only solution is to put up walls for yourself to keep the waves from passing through.

Let's suppose that my father was a real father who came home every night, that he bounced me on his knees, and had me listen to the tick-tock of his watch, let's suppose that he tucked me in and sang me lullabies at bedtime — there would still have been too many radio stations at the same time, and nothing would have been changed. I always began by talking about my father, because the psychologists liked that, as soon as I mentioned him they would wriggle contentedly in their chairs, they'd stop listening to me and try to explain what they'd learned in university, it was always interesting, really very interesting, the only trouble was that it had nothing to do with me, it explained nothing at all to me, and I didn't feel like going outside for five minutes a day to desensitize myself little by little, that wasn't my problem, my problem was that I heard too much, like Lindsay Wagner, so I arranged my life in my own way, that's all.

I've never liked street sounds, or the music they play in stores, even in my own kitchen I was careful when I was putting utensils away in the drawer, in fact you looked at my drawers and if you're at all observant you must have noticed that I'd put strips of cloth in the bottom, that's the proof, you see, I don't know many people who try so hard to eliminate excess sounds. It was the same when I played solitaire, I'd handle the cards very gently, there are people who can make a huge racket with a deck of cards and apparently it doesn't bother them, they feel more alive when they're making a noise, but for me it would be the opposite; I've always preferred silence, always, it wasn't a question of fear, not even fear of being afraid, I've never had anxiety attacks; all I wanted was to have some walls around me, to be able to choose my own radio station, just a little silence, that shouldn't be hard to understand, people can't all be the same … If I could talk to the doctors and psychologists, I'd tell them that I'm not the only one. Maybe each of us was isolated on our own side, in the days when we were down below, no one really paid us any attention, we were the lighthouse keepers, as you yourself said, Benoît, or monks who transcribed texts, cloistered nuns, shepherds, long-distance drivers, and housewives — thousands and thousands of housewives — but up here, we recognize one another and we know there are a good many of us, far more than I'd have thought, we're a large, silent army, the most innocuous of armies, the large army of lighthouse keepers, the army that will never make war, one that's content with operating the light to prevent ships from running aground, or to let children come home when night has fallen. We don't need to speak to understand one another, but it's reassuring to know there are so many of us, so reassuring that I don't even feel like going to visit other rooms, though I'm not sure you can talk about rooms because everything here is so big, maybe eventually I'll find a quiet little corner for myself, or maybe I won't need to, maybe each person makes his own paradise, just as he made his life, but I'm in no hurry, as you can see I'm taking my time, if I've spent my life exploring my kitchen I don't see why I shouldn't hang around in my corridor for a while. Be careful, Benoît, you're allowed yourself to be distracted but not too much, you've just turned over a ten of clubs when you could have put it on your jack of diamonds …

One day on the radio I heard a report by a man whose bones were so fragile he could hardly walk. No one would have asked that man to play football or become a boxer, correct? Did anyone suggest that he strengthen his bones, did they hit him with a stick to desensitize him little by little? Why should everybody be the same? I was someone who heard too much, or I was too sensitive to what I heard, I don't know. Maybe all children hear too much and then it's dulled, as happens with our sense of taste; adults are always complaining that nothing's the way it used to be when it's just their own taste that has dulled. They smoke cigarettes by the million, then complain that food doesn't taste the way it once did. Taste, sight, hearing, touch — everything becomes blunted, dulled, maybe it's the same for sensitivity, maybe some people started out more sensitive than others, and maybe sensitivity doesn't wear down at the same rate for everyone, maybe one day science will find a drug to numb sensitivity, if ever anyone figures out what it is and how to measure it. There are ways to test eyesight, but how can you know if one person is more sensitive than another? You can't measure tears, after all, and anyway tears mean nothing. Of a child who cries easily, you say that he's over-sensitive, when maybe he just has good tear glands, and I'm not sure that the person who reacts by delivering punches is any less sensitive. How can one person know what others feel, and how they feel?

I wasn't afraid of being afraid, learned Doctors, I was just too fragile, that's all. The good Lord forgot to issue me a carapace or to put filters in my ears, I'm not sure, either that or the sensitivity He gave me is the kind that doesn't dissolve with use. Some day I'll ask Him why He did that to me, even though I already have a pretty good idea of what His answer will be.

Everything I'm telling you, Benoît, I already knew when I was little, and everyone around me also knew. If your mother hadn't been there I don't think I'd ever have been able to go to school. Every morning, Cécile would start talking to me before we left the house, to reassure me; she'd say, don't listen to what you hear on the street, listen to me; she'd tell me stories, make me recite my catechism or my multiplication tables, she'd say just about anything to distract me — and it worked. At school, I'd go straight to my desk, I'd open my scribblers, and everything was fine, just fine: in those days the nuns knew how to impose silence; there were around forty of us little girls yet you could have heard a fly change directions, but that's just a manner of speaking, the nuns would never have tolerated a fly inside the classroom. You can't imagine how much I loved school, Benoît, you just can't imagine. At home we didn't have books, or newspapers, or magazines, or dictionaries, the only things that we had to read were FLOUR on bags of it and RED ROSE on the box of tea. Cécile cut out letters to teach me the alphabet, before I turned four she was already showing me how to read with the letters cut out from the box of RED ROSE tea, I can still remember the design — RED ROSE in big red letters and *orange pekoe* in black, and I also remember that my mother was grouchy whenever Cécile cut letters out for me.

Mama always used to say that she didn't like to read, or that it tired her eyes, or gave her a headache, she made up so many excuses that it got us thinking. The truth was that she didn't know how to read but was too proud to admit it. And she was unhappy when Cécile tried to teach me the alphabet: you'd better watch out, she'd say, it could put ideas in her head, as if there was nothing worse for a little girl than to have ideas … If it had just been up to my mother, I think I'd have stayed home all the time, and I certainly wouldn't have objected: I didn't like going out and it was not in my nature to protest. But Cécile was hardheaded, as I'm sure you know. She'd taken me under her wing and she had decided to take me to school, so I went to school and that was that. Once she'd made a decision, no one could stand up to her. No one even thought about it. She had *backbone*, as you would say.

So I went to school with Cécile. If she was sick and had to stay home, I was sick too, or so I pretended, and in the end I didn't even pretend: I waited until Cécile was back on her feet, that's all, and I couldn't wait till she was better, I was so anxious to sit there in silence, very straight, looking at books, opening dictionaries, and discovering words nestled tidily where they belonged. I've always liked words best when they're written down: they make less noise that way.

Sylvie was right when she said that the nuns were hopeless in English, so hopeless that I sometimes suspected they were doing it on purpose, but they were world champions in handwriting, that I'm sure of, and I've never lost my fondness for forming beautiful letters. I should talk to you about that a little, as a matter of fact, the children didn't tell you anything about that, it's as if they've forgotten how important it was to me, I'm sure you'll understand — with your own fondness for playing solitaire.

As you know, I've always liked playing solitaire too, it gave me something to do with my hands when I was listening to the radio, but there were times when I felt like doing something else, so I'd take a sheet of paper and my pen and I'd write my letters the way the nuns had taught me, perfect rows of capital *X*s — it's not easy to make capital *X*s, just try, you'll see, *K* is difficult too; I drew beautiful letters just for my own enjoyment — I'd have loved to be Chinese and have thousands of characters to learn — and I'd be concentrating so hard I'd sometimes forget about the radio. One year Daniel gave me a calligraphy set for Christmas. A pen-holder, an assortment of nibs, a bottle of ink, and an instruction manual; I could spend hours practising my downstrokes and my upstrokes, it was a good idea, Daniel was kind, but I don't understand why he told you about the birds I watched from the window and never about the letters I wrote, the birds were important, but not as important as the letters, which just goes to show that when we talk about other people we only talk about what interests us, but I'm not telling you anything you don't already know.

One day Sylvie asked me why I didn't write whole words as long as I was at it: why not sentences, stories, memories, thoughts? But it never crossed my mind that I might have anything to say, all I wanted was to concentrate on the letters. I was no artist, apparently. You ought to try it. It's even better than solitaire, you'll see.

I won't talk about all the things I liked, it would take too long, but I would like to say a few words, just a few about the radio: the radio I always listened to when I was drawing my letters and playing solitaire, that kept me company when I was washing the dishes or tidying my cupboards; I liked the serials well enough way back then, and it was such a letdown when they were adapted for television; what I imagined was a thousand times better than what I saw — in fact I wonder why they don't have them any more. Now it seems as if all you hear is songs, songs, and more songs, and hosts who have hysterics because the temperature has gone up two degrees or a carpet store is offering reductions; the worst of it is that they can't even wait for the song to be finished before they start shouting, I wonder how people can listen to them when it would be so easy to switch them off, it's a mystery. I simply couldn't listen to private radio, but the public radio was something else, I was addicted. They played songs that you never heard anywhere else, interviews with explorers who'd travelled to countries I knew nothing about, scientists who answered questions I'd never thought of asking, politicians who tried to solve those problems ... you can't imagine all the things I learned from listening to the radio; Marcel always used to say, *it's funny, I'm the one who travels, but you're the one with things to tell me when I come home*, and it's true, I really did learn a lot just by listening to the radio; the radio was my escape, my university, my woman friend, I don't know if the hosts know how important they are to us — the grand army of lighthouse keepers, and the sick, and the loners — I just wanted to take this opportunity to thank them, and while I think about it I'd like to talk to you a little about books, because people who write books may be lighthouse keepers too, lighthouse keepers who speak to shepherds or housewives, they don't come and shout in our ears, but that doesn't mean they have nothing to say, on the contrary: they put words where they belong, in drawers lined with cloth.

My fondness for books started when I was a girl, as we used to say back then — no one knew what a *teenager* was. After primary school, I went to the Institut familial to learn how to become a perfect wife. It was my own choice: I wanted to learn some really useful things, and above all I didn't want to have to take the streetcar like Cécile, who went to commercial school, and the Institut was close to home, I could walk there …

It was close to home, but Cécile still took the time to walk me there in the morning and to pick me up when school was out, and sometimes she'd have novels in her bag that one of her friends had lent her; she'd give me a wink as she pointed to her bag and I'd understand that we were going to have an evening of delights.

We'd go to bed a little earlier than usual, saying nothing to Mama because she was suspicious of books, we'd switch on a night light, then we'd read to each other in a quiet voice, which made it even more exciting. The stories we'd read were always set somewhere far away, in the Austrian court or the Arabian desert, the men were tall and strong, sometimes they had an ugly scar on their faces but they were still very handsome to anyone who knew how to love them, and they were so mysterious, I imagined them as being like big cats — jaguars or panthers … The heroines never did anything: they were content with having beautiful dresses and kind hearts. As soon as they met the prince or the sheik or the adventurer, lightning streaked across the sky and the world stopped turning; Cécile would swallow and her voice would be deeper when she read the beautiful words the authors had chosen to excite us, thrilling words like *turmoil, shudder, ecstasy, swoon* … As God is my witness, we didn't have the faintest idea about what pleasures those words were supposed to evoke, but oh my, it was good … I've never travelled except in books, and I've never regretted it. Good authors give us just the words we need and they take away the ones that aren't necessary; they choose the best radio stations and they remove the background noise; they anticipate everything a person doesn't want to see or hear. I continued to love books all my life, even if I didn't read so much at the end, because of my eyes. I loved books, but I think your mother loved them even more; in fact I think she loved them a little too much. I'd look at her sometimes, she'd bring her hand to her heart as if she wanted to contain her emotion, her eyes would get wet and there would be sobs in her voice, as if the heroine had *really* been abandoned by the handsome explorer ...

How happy Cécile would have been if life were like a novel, *but that's not the way it works, Cécile: a person can make the most beautiful sculpture, but there'll never be anyone else to pick up the shavings*, that was what I told her; *you have to bend over and sweep them up, we have no choice, and it doesn't mean that the sculpture isn't beautiful*, but Cécile was expecting people to talk the way they do in books, with no unnecessary words, with no shavings to sweep up, so she was disappointed, as you might expect, and, just between you and me, I think your father suffered a little because of it, but that ...

When she talked to me about her Prince, the one who would travel the world to find her, I told her, *Watch out, Cécile, there aren't many princes on the streets of Hochelaga, princes are fine in stories, in real life there are streetcar drivers and men who work for Vickers, and if that isn't good enough for you there are*

pharmacists, and doctors, and lawyers in offices on St. Jacques Street,
but Cécile wouldn't listen, she'd heave a great sigh, then she'd
turn over and go to sleep. She'd fall asleep with a sigh, and
that's not just a figure of speech, I really had the impression
that by sighing she was making herself a cloud in which she
felt protected. It was when she read love stories that Cécile
started to sigh, yes, I know what you're thinking, Benoît,
you're thinking that her sighs were just a way to load her
problems onto someone else's shoulders, but it was also a
way of communicating — awkward, maybe, but it was still
communicating, you may come to understand her one day.

I could hear too much, that was my disease. As for Cécile,
she hoped too much. She couldn't be content with a bus
driver, she needed more, much more ... I never wanted a
prince. I'd have been afraid of hurting myself on his medals
when I snuggled up to him. A bus driver was just what I
needed to keep me warm.

Cécile got married after I did, as you know. When she was
sure that I was properly settled, properly protected, she sat
out on the balcony and waited for a prince to appear on
Bennett Street, but it was your father who started taking
detours to go past her house, your father, who may not have
been a prince but he was a *businessman*, as Mama said, putting
on airs, *you aren't going to let a chance like that slip away, my girl*,
but you already know that story. What you may *not* know,
Benoît, is that your mother stopped reading novels the day
she got married, and I've never understood why; it was as if

life had become too real for her all at once; as if there'd been a great gulf between novels and real life, and that she was afraid of falling into it. She stopped reading novels, but she went on taking them out of the library for me, at least until I arranged something with my neighbour, but that's something else you know already, I don't intend to ramble on and on.

When your mother died I stopped reading too. It reminded me too much of the dreams we had as young girls. And then my eyes started not working so well. Even with large print it was hard.

Now, Benoît, now you're going to please me by starting a new chapter, you'll write the title in big print, on the centre of the page, and it will be a third love story. And I don't want any objections: this time, I'm the one who leads.

LOVE STORY, TAKE THREE

The nuns taught us spelling and beautiful handwriting, as well as sewing, piano, crochet, household science, and modesty — everything we'd need to become proper doctors' wives. In those days doctors didn't marry nurses, and they certainly didn't marry woman doctors, they looked for real wives, and becoming the wife of a doctor was a profession like any other — more attractive than many others too — and I had all the qualities needed to become a perfect doctor's wife: I was obedient and modest, I'd have just had to stay in school a while longer, be obedient till the end, till I got my diploma, then I'd have sat in the parlour and waited for Mother Superior to arrange a meeting. The nuns were excellent go-betweens: they would introduce you to a medical student in his final year, you'd serve him tea and cookies, play a sonata, even venture a bit of conversation though you didn't really have to, you would curtsy prettily and the deed was done. But I didn't complete my course. The nuns would have liked me to, but I stood up to them. I was a dropout as they say nowadays. I, Arlette, was a dropout … I hope you're impressed, and I hope that in future, you won't look down on me quite so much. That's right, I hope you won't look down on me quite so much, and I'm choosing my words carefully; you university teachers are sometimes contemptuous without realizing it, you look down on people, I imagine it's normal if you want to manufacture theories, but it seems to become second nature to think you're above other people, you have an aunt who became and remained a simple housewife and you give her the nickname Betty Crocker, you even claim that Betty Crocker has no backbone, well I'll have you know that Betty Crocker stood up to the nuns, which goes to show that it's not just your generation that had problems with authority. What's different is that we were more polite. I'm not here to preach, you're intelligent enough to understand, but even so, Benoît, even so, you'll forgive me if I spell it out, your remark about my backbone — rather, my lack of backbone — still sticks in my craw. I wasn't like some people who spend their lives moaning because the universe isn't exactly the way they'd have liked, it's true. Nor was I one of those who think the world should stop in its tracks because they've been born, that's also true. You've never seen me waving placards in the street, but that doesn't mean

I have no backbone, do I make myself clear? You may be a serious scholar, Benoît, but you've still got things to learn. You'll learn that backbone is not a question of quantity, and that an old dead aunt can still read over her nephew's shoulders, and allow me to add that I may not know much about etymology, but I'll bet as much as you want that the words envy and contempt come from the same country. There, I've said it.

If I'd stayed at the Institut another two months, I would have had my diploma. I was polite, obedient, and all that, I had high marks in all my subjects and I was in the good graces of Mother Superior, in fact she'd given me to understand that she would find the best match for me, but what happened was that Marcel came into my life by making strange sounds and here's the story.

They were three brothers who'd arrived straight from New Brunswick — you know the other two, they were at the funeral parlour — three brothers who'd come to look for work in the factories along the St. Lawrence, and they'd rented the apartment upstairs from us. We could hear them walk around, that's normal; we didn't live in a castle, it was just an ordinary house in a working-class neighbourhood, so we could hear some sounds from upstairs and soon we made a game of trying to guess what the three brothers were doing.

Rosaire always set out very early in the morning and came home a little before the others. We could hear his big boots on the stairs, thump, thump, thump, his steps were slow and even, you'd have said the paddles on a paddle wheel steamer, in fact he did work with boat motors; as soon as he got home he'd take off his big boots and my mother was very impressed: *men who live alone don't always remember to take off their boots when they come home*, she'd say, with her index finger raised, as if she were teaching us an important lesson in practical philosophy. The man took off his shoes when he came home. For her, that was the last word in chic.

So Rosaire was the first to come home from work, he'd take off his boots, then you could hear the floor creak all the way to the bathroom, after that he'd go to the kitchen, open and close drawers, cut up vegetables, chop chop chop, and we'd try to guess what he was making for supper. Eventually we learned that he made boiled beef on Monday, shepherd's pie on Tuesday, and so forth, but this we knew not just from the sounds we could hear, there were also the aromas that spread to all three floors of the house. Rosaire was an excellent cook, he bought spices at the Maisonneuve Market, spices that my mother didn't even know, and she couldn't get over it: *a man who cooks is rare enough, if he also thinks about something as sophisticated as spices, it's more than rare, it's ... it's ... it's ...* She had to start the sentence ten times, with her hand on her heart, and she never found a word that was stronger than silence. Which wasn't something that often happened.

Léopold would arrive half an hour later. He climbed the stairs a little faster, click, click, click, he wore hobnailed boots and he too took them off as soon as he was inside; after that we could hear him padding along to the bathroom, he always let the water run for a long time, even longer than the other two, and Mama nearly fainted: *on top of everything else they keep themselves clean!*

Marcel arrived last and we barely heard him. True, he was smaller than the others, but not that much, it's just that he walked on tiptoe and not on his heels; Marcel always tiptoed up the stairs, slowly, and he took the time to set his boots on the rug instead of dropping them — though it's also true that there wasn't as much room when he got home — he'd go to the bathroom, then into the kitchen where the others were waiting. We would hear them pull out their chairs, talk, sometimes even sing sea shanties, especially on fine summer evenings. Rosaire played the accordion, the others sang in harmony, and my mother would say that those men weren't drinkers because drinkers always sing off-key, and she was even more impressed, *men who don't drink, just think of it, girls, those men may just be workers but they're the cream of the crop*.

After that they'd listen to the radio, play cards and Parcheesi, then they'd go to bed. First Rosaire, whose room was at the front, in one half of the double living room, then Léopold, who slept in the middle bedroom, and finally Marcel, whose room was just above Cécile's and mine — did I tell you that she and I slept in the same bed? There was an expression back then, people would say that we were bed-sisters, I don't imagine anyone still says that nowadays.

Marcel sat on the edge of his bed, making the springs

creak, and right after that he started making his strange sounds. First a series of very regular tick, tick, ticks, as if he were dropping pencils on the floor, then we'd hear a kind of rumbling that grew more and more intense, sometimes lasting for a good half-hour; we kept asking ourselves questions, so many questions that we'd forget about reading our novels. No fictional plot could compete with that mystery which haunted us, night after night, and kept us awake, what on earth could they be, those tick, tick, ticks …

Mama finally couldn't take it any more. She ran into Marcel on the stairs and quite simply asked point blank, *tell me, what's the sound we hear every night from your bedroom, it doesn't disturb us, but it is intriguing*. Marcel turned red all the way to his ears, he said, *oh Lord, excuse me, I didn't think that it could disturb you* — afterwards my mother told us that he'd never looked so comical, with his big round eyes and his bright red face — and he finally explained that the sound was, *umm, well, it was … it was the sound of an electric train, I could show you if you like …*

She'd didn't need to be asked twice. She came to get us and the three of us went upstairs, like an official delegation; for us this was a big outing, an event, it would be the first time we set foot inside their apartment. Marcel took us to the living room, because it wouldn't have been proper for us to be in his bedroom, he got his electric train — meanwhile, Mama was pointing to the floor, and we realized what she was trying to tell us: the linoleum was so highly polished it was dazzling — then he came back with his box, he set up his train in the living room, we recognized the tick, tick, ticks of the rails when he set them down on the floor, then the rumbling of the motor. Marcel watched his train go around while I watched Marcel, and I thought he was so comical, he really did look funny with his big round eyes ...

Marcel always liked novelties. Whenever he came home from the States he'd bring us some new gadget, once it was an electrical machine for squeezing oranges, another time it was a battery-powered pencil sharpener that would swallow a pencil in ten seconds if you didn't watch out, every time he'd put his new treasure on the kitchen table, every time he'd watch it do its work, his eyes would fill with wonder, saying over and over how ingenious and smart it was, and the best thing was that he looked at his children the same way — that I learned later, of course, but already I could see that Marcel would be a good father.

When I watched him look at his train I knew right away that he was the one and there'd never be anyone else. Cécile went on reading novels and dreaming of sultans, but I didn't listen to her any more; I preferred to fall asleep to the whirring of the electric train.

After that, Marcel started making up all sorts of reasons to come down to our place; he'd bring strawberries from the market, or he'd want to make sure that his brother's accordion wasn't too loud, or he'd ask if there was any little thing that he could do for us, seeing as how three women on their own can't do everything, so Mama would ask him to repair all the electrical outlets in the house and I'd fall in love with him more and more.

Two months later, he asked for my hand. It was rather quick, but not that much. He knew what he wanted and so did I. At first Mama pretended to have some reservations, she said *he may be the cream of the workers, he's clean and all that, but he's still a worker, think about it, Arlette, and what will the nuns say …*

Cécile took my side right away. She said that Marcel may be a worker but that, first of all, he was a lot cleaner than plenty of doctors, and, secondly, he wouldn't stay a worker very long, because he'd soon be getting his bus driver's permit, and after all, a bus driver dresses better than a worker seeing as how he wears a uniform — Cécile always came up with the right arguments to sway Mama, because for her a diploma was just a piece of paper, whereas a *uniform*, now that's serious — *and thirdly, if Arlette has found the man of her life, we should be happy that she's going to marry him*, and she added new arguments all the way to tenthly, but Mama had long since made up her mind.

I left school before the end of the year and I never regretted it, even though I'd enjoyed school. *Nostalgia*, that's the first word you learn to laugh at when you come up here, the first word you forget. You can examine it up and down, you can't see what use it is, you can't even juggle with that word, you toss it in the air just once and right away, it vanishes. In fact it was with that word that I began to understand a little better how things work up here: first you examine all the words you know, one by one — the word *day*, for instance, or *nostalgia* — you take each one and manipulate it, massage it, and in the end you always find something strange about it, you juggle it a little and then you forget it — or maybe it's the word that forgets to fall back into your hands, I don't know. When words no longer serve a purpose, when you've forgotten them all, you move on to another stage. At that moment you can no longer communicate with anyone, of course, but apparently you no longer feel the need to, so it's fine.

The nuns had had their day and I never understood that so well as when the Beatles arrived. True, their songs were supposed to grate on the ears of women my age, but I thought they were so cute, so refreshing, even their sad songs put me in a good mood ... You wonder why I'm talking about the Beatles all of a sudden, maybe you don't think they have anything to do with our nuns, but that's not true, it sometimes seems to me that they've replaced the good sisters to a certain extent: beginning with the time when they started singing, no one wanted to walk around in a black gown, no one wanted to dress themselves up like a walking disaster. My own favourite Beatle was Paul. Mind you it's true that John seemed more intelligent, and George was more mysterious, and Ringo less pretentious, but Paul had a gift for describing ordinary people, like in "Eleanor Rigby," or "Penny Lane," or

"She's Leaving Home" ... John always told the others how to think, but it was Paul who could talk about a housewife in her kitchen and talk about her with respect. He knew how to look around him. And when he was young, he was so cute ...

But to get back to our subject. Marriage is a fine invention, but the marriage ceremony I could have done without, the honeymoon too, if you want to know what I really think.

I was afraid of the honeymoon, in fact, very afraid, to tell you the truth; I wasn't afraid of Marcel of course, but of the driving and the hotels and all that. It would be the first time I'd travelled so far — to Quebec City, just think! — the first time I would sleep in another bed than my own and with someone other than Cécile, the first time I would eat somewhere other than at home. I was afraid of everything, but I was with Marcel, and when I was with Marcel it was always fine: he drove so smoothly, he was the one who spoke with the waiters and the hotel staff, he always looked after me: I felt as if I were someone precious; on the road he'd tell me, look at this, look at that, but I wasn't really interested, all I wanted was to go home to Montreal. Marcel realized that quite quickly: we'd reserved the hotel room for a week but we came home after three days. Another man would have made a scene, another man would have harboured resentment, but Marcel was patient, he already knew that side of me, and to console me he said that everyone's afraid of something, for him it was needles, he couldn't look at one without fainting, even if it was just on TV he'd go pale, just hearing the word gave him the shivers, everyone has their fears, you see, and all you could do was talk about it with people you trust, so I could talk about it with him, which was something. The psychologists came later. Maybe they had such things in Outremont or Westmount, but in our neighbourhood we didn't even know such people existed, or if they did, they worked at the Saint-Jean-de-Dieu mental asylum; psychologists were for the rich or for real lunatics. The others got along as best they could, and I always found someone I wanted to get along with.

In the beginning, we lived in a little apartment on Adam Street, not far from Mama, you hadn't been born yet so you couldn't know, a tiny little apartment on the third floor, with a kitchen that looked out on the yard and a gallery that looked out on the lane, the women spent a lot of time on those galleries, often to hang out the laundry but also to sit and do nothing, to relax and chat, but I went out as seldom as possible, I even asked Marcel to move the clothesline closer to the door so I didn't have to go out very far. When I was with Marcel I was fine, he could always distract me, but when I was alone I started to hear too much, and that was when I began to live in my kitchen and create my own world for myself.

True, I was a little bored, I'd be lying if I denied that. When Marcel left for work I had a long day ahead of me and not much to do to keep busy; I found the time long, but that was normal, all women were like me, all women stayed at home; it wasn't up to the girls to visit the boys, as it says in the song, what girls did was sweep the house, so there was no question of going out to work; I did the housework and cooked the meals, I wrote down recipes I'd learned from the nuns, I played solitaire and did crosswords, but even so the hours were long.

Marcel always suggested I go out a little, get some fresh air, go shopping with my sister, or to the church basement where there were all kinds of activities for women, crocheting, sewing — but they were just to give your hands something to do while you gossiped and I didn't enjoy that; or I could have gone to the Saint-Vincent-de-Paul Society, mended clothes for the poor, that sort of thing, but it was always the same story — my ears were over sensitive and there was always too much noise and too many cars on the streets, and as time went on it got worse. Marcel was obliging, he always came shopping with me on his days off, in the evening I'd sometimes go to the library with Cécile, but most of the time I'd ask her to choose books for me and bring them to the house; Cécile was very obliging too, and that was how eventually I was able to accommodate myself to life.

Certainly I was a little bit bored, but eventually you learn how to enjoy the taste of boredom and as soon as I heard Marcel's footsteps on the stairs, I forgot I was bored. I was brand new, I felt good. He often suggested going for a walk, but I never wanted to, the only thing I could tolerate was going for long drives. He had every other Sunday off, and he always took Mama and me for drives; Mama loved going for drives, as soon as Marcel started up she'd begin to talk and she talked non-stop, maybe she imagined that her words served as fuel, or maybe it was her way of thanking the driver, whatever the reason she talked non-stop, and I'd look at Marcel from the corner of my eye, he was always smiling, always patient. As long as I was with him in the car it was fine, but I was still anxious to come home.

Did you know that was how your father won a place in mama's heart: he'd take her for long car rides and she was in seventh heaven ... I've often wondered if Cécile didn't wait a little too long before marrying; time has no respect for dreams, it continues to pass all the same, and it's always more cruel for a woman. Or maybe it was a little bit my fault too. Cécile would never have married before me, she'd have felt guilty at abandoning me; in her mind, she was responsible for her little sister and as long as I was there she couldn't be free. I could have managed though. Once I was married she really was free, but it took her a while to decide to get married herself, and she wasn't overflowing with enthusiasm; but I don't want to talk in her place, in fact I've already said too much, it's up to her to speak if she wants to.

I went to their wedding. I'd been preparing myself for it for months, Marcel stayed at my side the whole time, the two of us stepped inside the church, we sat near the door, and I was so uneasy, I saw nothing of the ceremony, I just tried to breathe deeply to calm myself, I tried to look at

Cécile's gown and listen to the priest's sermon, but it was hard; I've never liked churches, they're too big, too vast, if they want us to feel small then they succeed, but I myself always knew that I was small so there was no point in telling me every week, it was a waste of words; and then in a church the sounds always bounce around, someone ten rows ahead of you coughs and it's all you hear, I was embarrassed for the coughers, but that's not what I wanted to tell you, what I wanted to tell you is that while it's true I didn't go to your mother's funeral, I did go to her wedding, it took a tremendous effort, even though we came home right after the ceremony — we didn't go to the wedding banquet, that would have been too much to ask. Still, I can tell you that your mother was very beautiful that day, and that she looked happy, I can tell you that because it was there for all to see.

That was the last time I set foot inside a church, and the last time I got into a car to go somewhere other than the grocery store. I didn't miss it. Churches may be too big, but cars are much too small, you feel stifled in them, and besides they reek of plastic, which upsets my stomach, I wonder how people can stand it; every morning I listened to the traffic reports on the radio, even after Marcel died I kept doing it, the same with the weather, if there was a risk of a storm somewhere in the United States I knew about it, I always liked to know that kind of thing, I would listen when the reporters talked about traffic jams on the bridges, and I imagined a driver boiling inside his car, then he'd shut himself inside an office all day long, and in the evening he'd boil again on a bridge, and it's the same for everyone, including the woman on the radio who said that women were shut up in their kitchens and that they were prisoners there, I still resent her saying so, but I'll talk about that later.

While the drivers were baking inside their cars I was in my kitchen. True, the scenery I saw out the window didn't often change, but still there were birds that came and touched down on the window ledge, and the changing seasons, and the children riding around on their bikes, and the mailman ... You get used to the taste of boredom, as I told you before, but when you can see the time pass, you don't have the impression that it's doing something behind your back. I stayed in my kitchen, I did my crosswords, I looked out the window, I thought about Marcel out there in his bus, I followed him on a road map, and I would ask myself which of the two of us was more confined: maybe you assume I'm only saying that to justify myself, but think about it a little anyway before you decide.

Now, all my life I fixed meals for Marcel, of course, I looked after his clothes, I kept the house neat and clean so it would be welcoming. But don't forget that Marcel worked on the road, it would have been heartless for me not to do that, especially as I liked taking care of the house, and if you think about it I made more use of it than he did. I know that women rebelled during the sixties, and they were right; I also know that your mother was never so happy as when she went back to work, I don't dispute that; what I do dispute is the attitude of certain individuals, like that woman on the radio who called us brainless servants … It's not just university professors who look down on people, some people on the radio are good at that too. Maybe I have no backbone, but I do have a memory, as you can see. If I ever find out how to transform myself into a ghost, I can tell you there's one person who'll be hearing from me.

If my kitchen was a prison, I want you to know that no one ever locked me away there, especially not Marcel, it was the very opposite, in fact: he was the one who encouraged me to go out, who took me to see the doctors and psychologists when they started springing up all over; if I stayed in my kitchen it certainly wasn't his fault, and if Marcel took advantage of me then good for him, because I took advantage of him too, and now you're going to give me one last chapter because I want to tell you a little about the house in Boucherville; that's where I spent the most wonderful years of my life and I can feel now that my batteries are running down, so take me back to my kitchen for the last chapter, then it will be over, all I ask of you now is a little more patience.

THE CAT

It's true that our house in Beaurivage Gardens was beautiful, all white on its carpet of green, a house that was nearly new, but nearly new was even better than brand new, it meant that the work on the grounds had been done, the interior decoration too, the white broadloom I could have done without, but it would have been silly to waste it, and then there was the *finished* basement, as they used to say, and everything had all been done well, with good quality materials, I knew nothing about such things but Marcel's brothers had worked in construction for years and they gawked at the house, saying *now that's quality*, so we didn't ask too many questions and we bought it even though it was much too big for the two of us.

Now Marcel had things on his mind when he bought this house, as he told me later. First of all, he wanted me to have a big, beautiful, modern kitchen with a huge window facing south so I could take advantage of the light all day, but also to let me see what was going on outside, and what I saw was so much better than the lane on Adam Street: snow that stayed white all winter and nice green grass in the summer, a maple tree, a sidewalk where you hardly ever saw anyone except the mailman and children on their tricycles, so maybe I'd realize that there was nothing very dangerous outside, maybe I'd walk to the corner with him after supper; maybe we'd even venture two streets further, to see the ducks on the river; or even just go out in the yard, which was surrounded by a dense cedar hedge that was as opaque as a wall — Marcel always used to say that our yard was like a room added on to the house, we could have put up a picnic table and had our meals there in the summer; or maybe I'd be able to get to the carport, it was *part of the house, after all, look, Arlette, it's the same roof, we're outside but we're still safe* ... In the beginning I tried, I swear I tried with all my might, I'd sit on a lawn chair and Marcel always stayed with me, but every time, I found reasons to come inside and get something from the kitchen and then I wouldn't feel like going out again, so in the end he threw in the towel.

Right after we bought the house, a strange thing happened. For years we'd been trying to have children, unsuccessfully, and two months after we moved, that was it. We were like those couples who are sterile for years and then become fertile as soon as they adopt a baby. We aren't all that different from the animals, when you think of it: Marcel had found me a nest and as soon as I'd settled into it something happened inside me. I don't know if Daniel and Sylvie really were perfect children in a perfect house, as you've said so often, maybe there was a touch of irony in your remarks and if so, it's your problem; I don't know if they really were perfect children in a perfect house, but everything you said is true, they got their dose of Rice Krispies squares and hot chocolate, they took advantage of me as much as they could, which was quite all right because I took advantage of them too. Just the sight of them was my reward. I watched them grow and I enjoyed them, watched them go to school, overcome the childhood ordeals one by one, get on as best they could with their work and their love lives, and they always managed to surprise me. Those years were the most beautiful years of my life, I'm repeating it now and I'll repeat it as long as I still have the use of words — even afterwards if that's possible, and too bad for that woman on the radio.

I was lucky, when you think of it. When the children were very small, Marcel was there to take them to the playground, the pool, or the library. There were lots of children in those days, a number of mothers stayed at home, and they often gave me a hand, it was very convenient, especially for buying their clothes. After all, I couldn't make all their clothes myself, just try knitting nylon stockings, but I did sew for my neighbours, or I'd look after their children while they went shopping, and when they came to pick them up I'd serve them coffee and pie, we'd chat for a while, no one had any complaints and I never felt I was being exploited, a person can live her life in a kitchen perfectly well, there's nothing all that special about it, and it's certainly no worse than working in a mine and never seeing daylight.

The children left for school with their friends every morning, in the afternoon they came back with the same friends or others, there were so many children all over that I felt confident: the children looked out for each other, which reassured me. While they were at school I did my housework, and I swear that I didn't have time to be bored, people who want to be bored should never have children. The time passed quickly, so quickly, and the next thing I knew the children were gone and everyone on our street was old.

I liked everything about those years, everything, and one of the things I loved most was to entertain you all on New Year's Day; if you only knew how hard I worked to make a beautiful table, I wanted it to be as beautiful as a cover of *Good Housekeeping* and it was even better, I think. I didn't need to use soy sauce to make my turkey look perfect, I'll tell you my secret in a while if I have time, there were always cranberries and asparagus — for tradition but also for the colours — and plenty of stuffed olives, to echo the red and green of the tree, but on a smaller scale ... I took out the crystal glasses that had been a wedding present and the good silver, I put it all on my lace tablecloth that was as white as an artist's canvas ... One day I saw a report on TV about an artist who'd travelled the world with an exhibition, and her exhibition was precisely that: a table with plates, and on the plates a ceramic turkey and plastic peas; it was in the papers, if you can imagine, maybe she even got rich from her exhibition, I never really understood. That's what I did for my children every night, and on New Year's Day my table was a lot more attractive than hers, I'm not saying that to boast, it's a fact, you saw it yourself as far as that's concerned, I'm glad you mentioned it, Benoît, very glad, it makes up for the passage about my lack of backbone, and while I'm at it, I want you to know that those sandwiches without crusts — I only made them for you. I'd watch you stare at them greedily and that was my reward, you were brimming over with happiness and it was a beautiful sight. You always looked a little sad, but it was so easy to console you, I'd have been very foolish not to do it.

I was lucky, oh yes, I was lucky, and I thanked the good Lord every day. My children never had any illness more serious than mumps, Marcel was there to help when I needed it, the neighbours helped out too, and my children gave me a hand when they grew up — it took years for Daniel and Sylvie to realize that I never left the house, and when they finally did they were already used to it. And there was Cécile, always and ever after, and while I can't speak for her I can at least tell you what she did for me, maybe you were in the wrong position to understand, and I knew your mother, she never told you about it, so listen to me, just one last time, listen properly, then I'll go back to my kitchen and you'll never hear another word from me.

The errands that Cécile did for me at the other end of town you know about, the daily phone calls too; what you don't know is how helpful her stories and descriptions were when I started having trouble with my eyes. You know about that, Sylvie told you about it, and it's true, I should have had an operation for my cataracts, but while you can always find a GP who makes house calls, bringing out a specialist is another story, after all they can't move an operating room into a house, I realize that; everyone wanted me to have the operation but I'd have had to go out, and since I hadn't stuck my nose outside for twenty-five years I put it off again and again ... At first it wasn't too bad, things looked a little hazy, that's all; I stopped sewing, but I could always read, even if it was more tiring, I read in smaller doses, the same with my crosswords ... When such a change comes about little by little you get used to it, you can get used to anything, eventually, if there's one thing I've learned in my life it's that. When books are gone there's the radio, and even if your vision is blurred you can still distinguish the light, and even if there's hardly any light left, you can always talk to your sister on the phone and listen as she tells you about what's going on in her little world, all those small details that I tried to hold onto because they were important to me, because it was important to you, because life is nothing but details. When Cécile told me what was going on in your lives it was like a novel, a long novel that had started when we were little and was never interrupted. Now maybe Alexandre Dumas and Victor Hugo had more talent than Cécile, but she told stories well, your mother, she knew how to give just the necessary details so I could imagine the rest.

So there you go, you know the story, you'll tell it the way you want, but try to treat us respectfully, try to remind yourself that Patricia isn't the only one reading over your shoulder. Most of the time we prefer to be silent, but that doesn't mean we aren't there, or that you can't wound us without knowing it. There are millions of different ways to tell a story, you know that as well as I do. Sometimes, one word more or one word less or a shifted comma can change everything.

On television one day I saw a filmmaker showing us how one can work with light. He'd put a pretty girl in front of the camera and simply by moving the spotlights he made her ugly or fat or old or vulgar or mysterious. So just imagine what can be done with makeup and wigs. Just imagine filming that girl for two hours but only keeping two minutes worth of film. Anyone can become an angel or a devil, you just have to vary the camera angle, change a word or a comma ...

Cécile doesn't exist any more and I don't either. What's left of us is a story that each of us can tell in her own way. Cécile helped Arlette, Arlette helped Cécile. Cécile helped Arlette remain a prisoner, Arlette wanted to remain a prisoner and she needed Cécile. Arlette was a prisoner and Cécile was free, but Cécile was the prisoner of a prisoner who had chosen her prison freely. You just have to shift one word and everything changes. What's certain is that the two sisters no longer exist. What's left of them are the stories that everyone can tell in their own way, but you have to be careful with stories: sometimes they also become prisons. That's why most people aren't interested in becoming like those performers who desperately want to be talked about: they marry and the whole world has to know about it, they divorce and think the whole world will wipe away a tear. They become prisoners of their stories and then we wonder why they commit suicide. Normal people don't want to be shut away inside a single story, Benoît, especially not in a story told by someone else because that someone wants to deliver a message, or seem intelligent, or understand himself better, or I don't know what. I'm not the subject of a song, as Clémence Desrochers said about the girl who worked in the factory; I don't have grand ideas, I didn't have a grandiose life like the heroines of Cécile's novels; all I had was an ordinary little love story, a life in the suburbs, and that's all I left behind; I'm just a suburban housewife who waved to her children from the window when they left for school in the morning, and who was there again to greet them when they came home, a suburban housewife who made fudge and sandwiches without crusts, all I'm leaving is two children who grew up too quickly and who are still there, doing their best, that's all I

left and it's more than enough; I don't need to have everyone
know what I've done, what I've thought, or what I've said and
not said.

As I still have a tiny bit of energy left, I'd like to tell you
one last anecdote, but after that I'll ask you to leave me in
peace, Benoît, to let me rest. You've been kind and all that,
but now you should mind your own business. Don't ask me
why I'm finishing this way, we don't choose our memories,
you know that as well as I do, sometimes the camera freezes
on some insignificant detail, we don't know why we think
about it all the time when we forget much more serious
events; in my case what I think about all the time is a little
cat, a little cat that Daniel brought me one day, he'd bought
it for me, to keep me company, it was a wonderful idea, I
called him Felix the Cat, which wasn't very original, I know.
Felix was very young and already he wanted to go outside,
he insisted so much that I let him; what could happen to him
in our quiet neighbourhood, he'd go outside and play and
then he'd come home, so that day I let him out so he could
live his cat's life, and as soon as he got outside he started to
cross the street, so I called him and maybe that's what upset
his calculations, if I hadn't called him he would have had time
to get across, but I called him to make him come back and in
his cat's head he was all confused, so he stood in the middle
of the street and the inevitable happened.

After that I spent years and years feeling sorry, telling
myself that I shouldn't have called him: I should have let him

cross the street or kept him at home with me, apparently cats get used to that eventually ... I would have had to make a choice: either he stays or he goes, and there's nothing in between. Why do I still think about him, can you tell me? Why have I forgotten so many important things but not that? Why do I still see him crossing the street and not deciding, not knowing which signal to listen to?

Now look both ways before you cross the street, Benoît. And cover up. Take care.

ACKNOWLEDGEMENTS

Thanks to Pierre Laliberté, Louis Auger, Patricia Pitcher, Marie Pelletier, and Lucie Mercier, who were kind enough to talk to me about their professions, and to Pierre Petit, who introduced me to Beaurivage Gardens.

Some of Benoît's ideas are inspired by an article by Laurier Lapierre entitled "Le ménagement: ménager, faire le ménage et se ménager," which was published in *Gestion* in November, 1992.

The book *Madame et le management*, by Christiane Collange, really does exist. It was even re-released by Arthème Fayard in 2002.

Thanks as well to Jean-Marie, Suzanne, Sheila, Normand, Isabelle, Charles, Anne-Marie, and Michèle for helping me do the necessary housework in the manuscript — and for much else.

ABOUT THE AUTHOR

François Gravel is the author of more than twenty-five books, including the novels *A Good Life*, *Miss September*, *Ostend*, and *Felicity's Fool*, all of which have been translated by Sheila Fischman and published by Cormorant Books. He has been nominated for many awards and prizes, including le Prix du Journal de Montréal, the Brive-Montréal Prize, and the Alvine-Bélisle Award. He has won the Governor General's Literary Award for Children's Literature for *Deux heures et demie avant Jasmine*, published in English as *Waiting for Jasmine*. He lives in Montréal and teaches at the Collège Saint-Jean-sur-Richelieu.

François Gravel is the author of a number of novels, of which the following have been translated by Sheila Fischman:

Benito (1990, Lester &Orpen Dennys)
Felicity's Fool (1992, Cormorant Books)
Ostend (1996, Cormorant Books)
Miss September (1998, Cormorant Books)

A Good Life (2001, Cormorant Books)
The Extraordinary Garden (2005, Cormorant Books)
Adieu, Betty Crocker (2005, Cormorant Books)
Waiting for Jasmine (1993), for young adults, available from
    Groundwood Books

In the French language, he has published the following novels:

Adieu, Betty Crocker (2003, Québec Amérique)
Benito (1987, Boréal)
Bonheur fou (1990, Boréal)
Corneilles (1989, Boréal)
Fillion et frères (2000, Québec Amérique)
Granulite (1992, Québec/Amérique)
Guillaume (1995, Québec/Amérique)
Je ne comprends pas tout (2002, Québec Amérique)
La note de passage (1993, BQ)
L'Effet Summerhill (1988, Boréal)
Les Black Stone vous reviendront dans quelques instants (1991,
    Québec/Amérique)
Mélamine Blues (2005, Québec Amérique)
Miss Septembre (1996, Éditions Québec/Amérique)
Ostende (1994, Éditions Québec/Amérique)
Sekhmet (2005, Québec Amérique)
Zamboni (1990, Boréal)

Poetry:

L'été de la moustache (2000 Les 400 coups)
Voyage en Amnésie et autres poèmes débiles (2004, Les 400 coups)

ABOUT THE
TRANSLATOR

Sheila Fischman is the award-winning translator of literary works by Marie-Claire Blais, Roch Carrier, Michel Tremblay, Anne Hébert, Gaétan Soucy, Christiane Frenette and Élise Turcotte. She has won the Canada Council Translation Prize (twice), the Governor General's Literary Award for Translation, and the Félix Antoine Savard Prize (twice). In recognition of the excellence of her work and of her contribution to the cultural life of Canada, Sheila Fischman was named to the Order of Canada in 2000.

Born in Saskatchewan, raised and educated in Toronto, she has lived in Montreal for the past thirty years. Sheila Fischman was the literary editor of *The Montreal Star* in 1977, but now works full-time as a literary translator. Together with D. G. Jones, she founded *ellipse*, the literary magazine of translation. She was one of the founding directors of the Quebec Society for the Promotion of English Language Literature, of which the QSPELL Awards (now the Quebec Writers' Federation Awards) were the most public activity. She was also a founding member of the Literary Translators' Association.

Sheila Fischman has translated over one hundred literary books, including the following:

The Alien House, *The Body's Place*, and *The Sound of Living Things*, all by Élise Turcotte

The Whole Night Through and *Terra Firma*, both by Christiane Frenette

Wild Cat, *Autumn Rounds*, *Mr. Blue*, *Volkswagen Blues*, *Spring Tides*, and *The Jimmy Trilogy*, all by Jacques Poulin

The Fat Woman Next Door is Pregnant, *Thérèse and Pierrette and the Little Hanging Angel*, *A Thing of Beauty*, *Birth of a Bookworm*, *Bambi and Me*, among many others, by Michel Tremblay

The Wolf, *A Literary Affair*, *Anna's World*, and *These Festive Nights*, all by Marie-Claire Blais

Atonement, *The Little Girl Who Was Too Fond of Matches*, *Vaudeville!*, and *The Anguish of the Heron*, all by Gaétan Soucy

Héloise, *In the Shadow of the Wind*, *Am I Disturbing You*, *The First Garden*, and *Burden of Dreams*, among others, by Anne Hébert

La Guerre, *Yes Sir!*, *The Hockey Sweater*, and all of the adult fiction, as well as four children's books, by Roch Carrier